The Black Stallion Challenged!

Scarcely a day went by when Alec Ramsay, owner of the famous Black Stallion, wasn't deluged with fan mail. But the letter from a boy named Steve Duncan was different.

Steve, too, owned a horse—"the fastest runner in the world," he wrote, "faster than the Black. I want to race Flame. Will you help me?"

Faster than the Black? Alec found Steve's blind confidence in Flame very irritating. But when Flame and the Black had their first run together, Alec had to admit that the Black had finally met his match. And when the two fabulous stallions met in a major race, the whole world wondered if the Black could hold his own against the upstart challenger. . . .

The Black Stallion Challenged!

by WALTER FARLEY

RANDOM HOUSE  NEW YORK

Library of Congress Cataloging in Publication Data
Farley, Walter
The black stallion challenged!
New York, Random House [1964]
I. Title   PZ10.3.F22B11   64-15094
ISBN: 0-394-80617-4 (trade hardcover)
       0-394-90617-9 (library binding)
       0-394-84371-1 (trade paperback)

For Elizabeth Ingersoll
whose encouragement and advice have
meant so much to me throughout
the years

Contents

The Black Stallion Challenged!

Fan Mail

1

"*Dear Alec Ramsay,*" the letter began, "*I've wanted to write you a long time but was afraid you'd be too busy even to read my letter. I finally decided I just had to take a chance and write anyway. I know there's no one else who would understand my love for a horse as much as you and I need your help very much.*"

Alec stopped reading and got off his seat on the tack trunk so the old man with him could rummage inside. "What are you looking for, Henry?" he asked.

"The x-ray plates Doc Palmer took," the trainer said.

"The latest batch?" Alec asked.

"Yeah, those."

"In the right-hand corner."

Removing the stack of negatives, the old man held them up to the morning sunlight coming through the doorway of the small room. He stared at the x-rays, shook his head, then climbed up on the tack trunk and held the negatives against the bare light bulb.

"You won't find anything," Alec said. "You never do."

"There just might be a speck we missed."

"There's nothing," Alec insisted. "The Black's hoof

3

healed long ago. We have the doc's word for it. We have clean pictures and we know he's acting right." Mounting impatience with the old man made him add, "I don't see why you keep looking for trouble, Henry. He was wild to run this morning. I haven't seen him act so alive and well in months."

"You let him get away from you," the old man said defensively. "You were supposed to take him for a sightseeing gallop and you didn't."

"I couldn't. As I say, he was wild. He felt good. He was bucking and playing all the way. You know yourself that he was still so fresh when we got back to the barn that it took the two of us to walk him."

"I know," the old man said, still studying the pictures.

Alec Ramsay turned back to the letter in his hand. "You want me to read this letter to you?"

"Why not? Don't you always read your fan mail to me?"

"But sometimes you don't listen."

"I'll listen. I can work at the same time." Henry Dailey held the x-ray negatives to the light bulb again and added, "Whoever is writing needs your help. Like maybe ten others a week you hear from. He loves horses as much as you do. Or maybe it's from a girl this time?"

Alec turned over the letter to read the signature. "No, it's from a fellow. Someone named Steve Duncan. But you're right so far . . . he loves horses as much as I do and he's asking for help."

"Want me to go on?" the old man asked without taking his eyes from the negatives. "I can tell you the rest of it, almost word for word."

"No, let me read it to you. Maybe it'll be different this time." But different or not, Alec decided it was good knowing people were interested enough in him and the Black to write. If the day ever came when he and Henry became too busy to read such letters, it would be time to quit racing altogether.

"From the newspapers I know you have the Black at Hialeah Park this winter and may race him before long," Alec read aloud. *"I know exactly how you feel having such a wonderful horse and I wish . . ."*

Henry stepped down from the tack trunk, replacing the x-ray negatives in a large manila envelope. "That fellow knows *exactly* how you feel having the Black, and he wants one *exactly* like him someday," he said. "You're not going to be able to help him any more than you did the others, Alec. How come people don't understand that a truly great horse like the Black turns up just once in a lifetime, if at all?"

Alec shrugged his shoulders as he met the old man's gaze. Henry's face had the texture of old parchment crisscrossed with a mass of wrinkles, but his eyes and voice still held the fire and gusto of youth.

"I'd pity most of them if they ever *did* have a horse like the Black," the old man went on. "They don't know what it's like having a great horse on their hands. They don't know any of the *problems*."

"Who're you kidding? You wouldn't change it for the world, Henry," Alec said.

"Of course not. I waited all my life for the Black to come along. Maybe I worry about him too much, like you say," he went on. "Sometimes I think he's going to worry me to death. Sometimes I can't eat or sleep, just knowing I got the *big one* in my stable. That's the way it is, but I wouldn't wish it on anyone else."

Turning back to the letter, Alec said, "This fellow seems to have something else in mind."

". . . *and I wish*," he continued reading, "*that you and I could get together. I live in Miami now. My family moved here from the North last fall. It would be easy for me to get to Hialeah to see you. Would you mind if I came over soon? It's very important and I'm sure you could help me*."

"That's great, just great," the old man said. "All we need around here is a horse-struck kid with a problem. Maybe he won't get past the barn gate."

"That doesn't sound like you, Henry," Alec said. "It won't do any harm to see him if he does come. I don't see what's wrong with you these days. You're too cautious about everything."

Henry straightened his blocklike figure, making a gallant attempt to look unconcerned at Alec's criticism and regain his position of authority. He didn't like the way Alec was sizing him up. Alec was too composed while Henry was squirming inwardly. Maybe it was a sign of old age creeping up on him. Maybe it wasn't a case of being as old as one felt but as old as one *was*.

"I guess you're right," he said finally. "I didn't mean it the way it sounded. We'll help him all we can."

Alec smiled, trying to make it easier for his old friend. He thought he knew how the trainer felt. The Black had made up for a lot of disappointments in Henry's long life. Despite his ever-present anxiety over the Black's soundness, Henry was a happy man.

Having a great horse could make anyone really enjoy life to the fullest.

"Do you want me to go on?" Alec asked, turning back to the letter.

"Is there much more?" Henry asked with mounting impatience. He tried to meet the youth's gaze and failed miserably. Finding himself stooped over, his arms hanging down like an ape's, he straightened quickly. "Sure, go ahead," he said brusquely.

Alec continued reading. "*I realize you must hear from many fans who would like to meet you. So I must convince you that this letter is different from the others.*"

Henry groaned and shifted his weight from one foot to the other. Once again he was ill at ease because Alec was looking at him. He knew the youth could penetrate any thought he might want to keep to himself, and what he was thinking now made him seem like an utter fool. Why in the world should he be disturbed by a letter from a youngster that was no different from hundreds of others Alec had received? Or was his uneasiness caused by a strong feeling that this letter was going to prove different?

"Well, you know what I mean, Alec," he said finally. "All these kids seem to think their particular problem is more important than anyone else's. It gets kind of annoying, especially when we have so much work to do."

"Okay, Henry," Alec said, starting to fold the letter and put it away. "I'll finish it later."

"Finish it now if you like," Henry said. "But let's get some work done too."

Alec rose from the trunk. "What do you want done?" he asked.

"I want to check his foot again," Henry said. "Get me the small tongs."

While Alec searched the trunk for the pair of tongs, Henry studied him. It was really quite remarkable that Alec was essentially the same kid he was years ago when they'd first met. This, despite the fact that he was now one of the nation's top jockeys. There were few riders around who could match his skill on the race track.

He studied the youth as he bent over the tack trunk. Alec still weighed only about one hundred and ten pounds and most of the weight was in his arms and chest, making him look like sort of a husky bulldog— except for his face, of course. Alec had a thin, good-looking face, unlined and set off by prominent, even teeth that flashed whenever he smiled, which was a good bit of the time. His hair was more red than ever due to the long time he'd spent in the sun. There were a few strands of hay hanging from his white T-shirt, and his blue Levis looked much too hot for Florida weather. Few would have taken him for the successful young rider he was.

When Alec turned to him, the tongs in hand, Henry said, "Take some of that hay off your shirt and out of your hair. You look like you just rolled out of a stall."

"I did," Alec said, smiling. "I find I'm spending most of my time there."

"No need to be untidy, even if you are tending a horse," the old man answered. But he knew that if Alec was untidy, it was not through inclination but rather that sometimes he was too impatient to take time to clean up. Alec was always in a hurry, always working at new ideas.

"Come on," Henry said, starting for the door.

It was late morning and the quiet around the stable area was almost tangible. But within an hour or two the barns would come to life again, and shortly thereafter the cries of the afternoon racing crowd would be heard beyond Hialeah's towering royal palms and Australian pines.

Outside the tack room, Henry stopped to remove the floppy straw hat he wore constantly to shield his head and face from the hot Florida sun. He brushed a bare arm across his forehead to remove the perspiration, then glanced skyward toward the south where the clouds were darkest and held some promise of rain to cool things off.

Alec said, "If the heat bothers you, just remember there are eighteen inches of snow in New York City alone."

"I know. I saw it on TV this morning. New York could have been Nome, Alaska, the way it looked up there. Cars and buses buried in snow. Airports shut down. It looked real ghostlike."

"And cold," Alec said. "Real cold, two degrees above zero. It's the sixteenth day below freezing they've had."

"The snow and cold I could take, maybe. But not the gales. High winds seem to go right through me these years."

"Then it wasn't such a bad idea spending the winter here?"

"Not so bad."

Alec smiled. Henry might be the bright-eyed, hard-eyed trainer of old but his friends at the northern tracks would hardly approve of his clothes. At least they weren't in keeping with the Henry they'd known. In addition to the floppy straw hat, he wore a red cotton shirt and gray-flecked pants. His gray hair was close-cropped, too, in keeping with his Florida attire. Altogether it made him look younger than he was. He'd sweated off some weight too, now being more portly than fat.

Alec noted a slight, sickly pallor beneath Henry's heavy, leathery tan. It was enough to cause him some concern, for his old friend had not been sleeping well.

"You feel all right today?" he asked cautiously.

"Sure. Why not?"

"I thought you might want to rest awhile. I can finish up." Alec started to say more, shrugged his shoulders and clamped his lips together. He'd started enough things today without getting into any further arguments with Henry.

"Don't you worry none about me, Alec," the trainer said. "I'm fine. I don't need as much sleep as I used to. Besides, racetrack people are known to be tough and long-lived. You know that as well as I do. It's all the fresh air we get."

"You sound as if you're trying to convince yourself of your good health," Alec said quietly.

The trainer didn't answer. He walked down the shed row with a smoothness and certainty to his gait that were surprising in a man so heavily built. Just ahead was a stall with a large gold star over the door, which Hialeah Park had furnished to indicate the domicile of a champion. Sticking his head out of the stall was the Black Stallion, his powerful shoulders shoved against the webbing across the doorway.

"There's the old boy now," Henry said.

Old boy nothing, Alec thought. The Black acted as young and fractious as any colt. If one didn't know this horse, he'd have to be mighty careful how he approached him. The Black inspected friends and visitors alike as if he were a bird of prey, ready to swoop down on them from great heights. The tall stallion whinnied and shook his head in greeting, the muscles rippling beneath his black sable coat.

There was an unmistakable glow of health about him which prompted Alec to say again, "You won't find anything wrong with his foot, Henry. Even if we were going in a horse show, he'd be the winner."

Henry went into the stall without answering and Alec followed quietly, cautioning himself to hold his tongue, to play it wise. He should know by now how best to handle Henry. Slipping on the Black's halter, he held the stallion in readiness for Henry.

"Give me the tongs," Henry said.

The trainer raised the Black's left foreleg. It was cold to the touch, as it should have been. He went over the raised foot with the small tongs, closing the jaws of the instrument at different parts. The horse never flinched. There was no sign of sensitivity from the old injury, yet Henry said, "Never can tell. There might be a nerve pressing somewhere."

"He'd have come back lame this morning, if there was," Alec answered. "I think he's as fit as he'll ever be." He hadn't meant to say anything. It had come out before he could stop himself. When Henry glanced up at him, Alec squared his shoulders and made a gallant attempt to look unconcerned, as if it didn't matter to him whether or not the Black ever raced at Hialeah Park. He held the old man's gaze without flinching.

Henry said critically, "You got any idea how many horses stay sound during their racing careers, Alec?"

Alec shook his head.

"Just one-tenth of them," Henry answered. "Only one-tenth of all the thousands racing. Remember that figure. And I aim to keep the Black sound."

"You have," Alec said.

"I think he has an excellent chance of being ready to race, Alec, if that's what you're driving at," Henry went on. "I guess I'd be as disappointed as you if he's not ready sometime this month. But there are things you can't control, so we have to be on our guard every minute. When you have a horse like the Black, you don't want to take any chances racing him when he's not perfectly fit."

Alec nodded, his eyes turning again to the Black, who had stopped stalking his stall to munch hay from the corner rack. Henry was right, of course. Only a few months ago it was rumored throughout the racing world that the great champion had broken down. Now he was on his way back and he looked superb, as fit as a horse could be. But was he? Would the injured foot hold up under the pounding it must take when he raced? For a moment Alec stood beside his horse in troubled silence.

Henry said, "We'll just keep giving him long, slow

works for the time being. If he continues to go well, as we hope he will, and his condition is as good as it should be, he'll race. Otherwise, he'll stay in the barn and we'll have spent a nice quiet winter in sunny Florida. As you said before, that's not too bad."

The old man put his arm around Alec's shoulders. "Don't worry about it," he said, hoping to cheer up his young friend. "You'll get your race yet. I know how you feel."

Alec turned away, trying to conceal his disappointment.

Watching him, Henry wondered if he really *did* understand Alec's mounting impatience to race the Black. Alec lived in a different world, one that he himself had not known in a long time and one he would have completely forgotten had it not been for their close friendship.

"Alec," he said, peering at the youth from beneath his heavy brows, "maybe we can race the Black sooner than I thought. And why don't you read the rest of that letter you got? What else does that young fellow have to say, anyway?"

Alec said nothing for a moment. He just watched as his old friend stood there, fretting and massaging his cheeks with one hand. Then, "You mean you really want to know?" he asked.

"Sure," Henry said, a slight, patient smile crossing his face. "Maybe we, I mean *you*, can give him a hand at that. Maybe it'll even do you some good to have a young fellow around . . . one with a problem, I mean."

When Alec's hand went to his pocket for the letter,

the Black Stallion bent his long, graceful neck, his nostrils quivering and sniffing.

Alec told him, "I have no carrots, not now."

The Black remained still, his long tail swishing contentedly but not a muscle moving beneath his velvet-soft coat. His gaze had turned to the open doorway and, with his ears cocked, he was listening to low-pitched sounds from the stable area.

Alec's eyes remained on him. Never was there a more magnificent horse than his own. He was a perfect specimen, perfectly balanced, perfectly mus-cled. And he was as intelligent as he was well-made.

Alec returned to the letter and read to Henry, *". . . I must convince you that this letter is different from the others. The only way I know how is to tell you what I've never told anyone else, not my mother or father or closest friends. Even if I did I don't think they'd believe me. Neither will you, perhaps—yet I hope it will surprise you enough to see me."*

Henry said, "Pretty dramatic, isn't he?"

Alec glanced up. "He sounds pretty serious to me."

"Yeah, I know," Henry said. "Go on."

"I have a horse . . ."

"That's a relief," Henry interrupted again. "At least he doesn't need our help in getting a horse. That's different from most of the others for sure."

Alec's eyes didn't leave the letter.

"His name is Flame," he read. *"I think he is the fastest horse in the world!"*

"That's good," Henry said. "Everybody's horse should be the fastest in the world."

"Faster than the Black."

"That's new," Henry said. "Your fans usually don't go so far as to say that."

"Not long ago I clocked him a mile in 1:34."

"He almost broke the world's record," Henry said, smiling. "He must have been carrying an alarm clock."

"Over a turf course," Alec went on.

"That makes it real wild," Henry said, grinning broadly now. "What an imagination this fellow's got!" He started for the stall door. "You've got an imagination to match his, Alec. You better finish reading it yourself. My mind's too lazy to keep up with stories like that."

"I want to race my horse at Hialeah," Alec read quickly before Henry could leave. *"Will you help me?"*

Henry had reached the doorway, but now he turned around. He said nothing. He just laughed, and his laughter could be heard long after he'd left the stall and was on his way down the shed row.

Alone, Alec re-read the letter. A fellow by the name of Steve Duncan owned a horse named Flame, a horse he claimed could run a mile in world-record time. He wanted help in getting him to Hialeah to race.

It sounded pretty fantastic, except that Alec well recalled his own beginning with the Black. That, too, had been hard to believe. Such a story as Steve Duncan's demanded an imaginative effort which Henry did not care to extend. It was different with Alec. His mind was not lazy. He looked forward to meeting Steve Duncan and his horse Flame.

The Visitor

2

Alec snapped the lead shank to the Black's halter. He never liked to keep his horse in a stall too long. The Black was a lover of freedom. He thrived best on the blowing wind and green grass.

"Easy," Alec said. The Black was already on his toes, knowing where he was being taken. As he left the stall, the sun brought out the highlights of his finely brushed coat. There was no fat on him. Nor did he look drawn, creased or worn-out. There was a sharpness and spring to every movement that matched the alertness in his eyes. Alec knew he was in perfect racing condition regardless of what Henry had told him.

They walked through the quiet area, many of the stabled horses snorting and whinnying as they went by. Alec would have liked to walk every horse there. If all of them had the opportunity to pick grass in the open air, they'd be less likely to turn sour and sulk. As it was, most of the horses were kept in their stalls except when they were on the track and, as a result, were either too nervous or bad-natured.

Alec would have preferred turning the Black loose in an open paddock as he and Henry had done at

Belmont Park in New York. But letting him graze on a lead shank was the best that could be done in Hialeah's cramped stable area.

The Black walked on long, springy pasterns, his legs set well beneath him. Suddenly, he bolted forward as if wanting to be free. Alec spoke to him and he stopped, cocking his small ears and listening. Then he whinnied in reply, his long nostrils distended, his eyes bold. The Black was well loved by Alec and he knew it.

Alec thought he had the sharpest horse in the world, and he was anxious to take on all those who would challenge his championship crown. As the veterinarian had said, "I don't mean the Black is just racing sound, Alec. He's *completely* sound."

Henry had been almost convinced by those words. Almost, but not quite. Henry was a worrier. Henry never had intended to race the Black this winter, Alec was certain. But their horse had gotten so tight at Hialeah that the wisest thing to do *was* to race him. Otherwise, they might get into real trouble. Like a drum or a bow, a horse would break if drawn too tight. There had to be some release.

The Black had been away from the races a long time now. But Alec had only to look at him to know he had not forgotten how it had been. There was no doubt in Alec's mind that a noticeable change had come over his horse once he had achieved success on the race track. Perhaps it was the roar of the crowd, or the rush of other horses alongside. Whatever had accounted for it, it had happened. And if Alec had anything to say about it, not only the public but he, too, would thrill

again to the Black's closing rushes down the homestretch. It was time his horse went after championship
honors once more. Hialeah, early in the new year, was
a good place to start.

At a grassy area near the outside fence, he let the
Black graze. But his thoughts turned to Henry again,
for it was the trainer who would decide if the Black
was to race. To most people his old friend was the
hard-hearted horse trader of legend, but Alec knew
that, deep within, Henry was still pretty much of a
country boy, shy and warm, loving both horses and
people. Henry had earned his reputation for tough-
ness in his dealings with other horsemen, who were
also tops in their business. You never fooled any of the
old professionals twice. You never got the chance.

Henry had said a little while ago that they might
race the Black sooner than he'd thought. That was
good enough for the time being. Now, there would be
more meaning to their morning gallops.

Alec turned back to his horse. Something had
disturbed him, for he had stopped grazing and his
head was raised. His nostrils quivered, and there was
a nervous twitching of his ears. A sudden gust of wind
riffled his mane and tail.

Just looking at him gave Alec a queer feeling in his
stomach. It had been that way from the very beginning. As with a lot of other things, there was no use
trying to explain his feelings to anyone else. It just
happened, when you had a great horse. The power in
the Black was unbelievable, but you had to be on his
back to really appreciate it. He always seemed to be

running beautifully. Then, suddenly, he would take off and stretch out until you were sure you were flying! Unless you rode him you couldn't know the feeling, and that was why Alec couldn't explain the way he felt about the Black to anyone.

"What is it?" Alec asked his horse.

The Black's nostrils continued working, sniffing the upwind, inhaling and exhaling without snorting or whinnying. The stable area was silent but the moving air carried some sort of news to him.

"What is it?" Alec asked again.

The Black had been born free, so Alec knew better than to discount his natural instincts. He was all stallion—strong, arrogant and, at times, very savage and cunning. He continued searching the air for some kind of scent.

Alec turned with his horse, surveying the solitude of the stable area and finding nothing. He looked again at the Black, becoming a little uneasy, for it had been a long time since he had seen his horse act quite like this.

The stallion's eyes, large and black and brilliant, were unmoving, and the air about him seemed to come alive with invisible fire.

Alec spoke to him softly.

The Black began to breathe harder, the sides of his chest moving in and out faster and deeper while Alec talked to him. He seemed to be listening to what Alec had to say, for one sharp ear was turned toward him while the other remained pricked in the direction of the barns.

Alec, still talking to him, gave the lead shank another twist.

With head raised high, the Black continued to survey the area. Then, suddenly, his nostrils turned slightly red as he blew them out, snorting. His great eyes bulged from their sockets, all thunder and flame, and his lips were drawn back, disclosing raking teeth.

The quiet of the stable area was shattered as he screamed his high-pitched clarion call. It was a wild, shrill whistle, the savage challenge of one stallion to another!

When the sound of it died down, there was no answer to his sudden, unaccountable challenge. A few of the stabled horses snorted, but they did so more in fear than in acceptance of a battle, for their lives were completely domestic. None bore the scars of battle as did the Black. It had never been their lot to fight in a contest of strength or in anger or jealousy.

Alec waited for his horse to plunge forward as he was sure he must after uttering such a wild scream. He braced himself, snubbing the end of the long shank around his body. But the Black never moved. His gaze remained fixed on a distant row of stables.

Yet nothing happened. No one moved. No one came. The minutes passed, then finally the Black tossed his head and uttered a high, bugling snort. When there was still no answer, he seemed to lose interest entirely. Quickly, he lowered his head and began snipping the grass again with his sharp teeth.

"Never a dull moment with you," Alec said, grinding his teeth. "Never."

What had caused such a commotion? he wondered. For a few minutes the Black had become all stallion, a *herd* stallion, ready to defend his mares against another stallion.

Snorting, the Black raised his head again. This time there was somebody coming toward them. From a distance the youth appeared tall but as he got closer Alec saw that he was no taller than himself. It was his slimness—for he was almost all skin and bones—which gave the illusion of height. He wore a black suit, a white shirt and a dark tie.

He came directly toward them, and the Black watched him all the while, his nostrils blown out and working again. When the youth stopped before them, he said, "You're Alec Ramsay. I wrote you a letter. I'm Steve Duncan."

"I guessed as much," Alec said. The boy's hair was coal-black and brushed, as slick as the rest of him.

A baffled expression came over the youth's face. "How come?" he asked.

"I wasn't expecting any other visitor," Alec said. "And I'd just finished reading your letter. How'd you get through the barn gate?"

"I told the guard I was the son of an owner."

"Yes," Alec said, quietly. "You could be."

Suddenly, Steve Duncan's black eyes were flashing fire. "The next time," he said, "it will be different. I won't have to lie to get in here." His tanned skin was stretched tight over the bones of his face.

"I'm sure you won't," Alec said, surprised by the other's outburst. He found himself enjoying Steve

Duncan's intentness, his ingenuity, even his excitability. It was a nice change after dealing with Henry all morning.

"The next time I come," the youth went on, "everybody will be glad to see me. I'll bring Flame and—"

"Sure," Alec said, interrupting. "But the first thing you've got to learn is not to get so excited."

"I don't get excited, not when I'm riding," the other answered quickly.

"It's nice to keep your mind on it all the time," Alec said.

"I'll do okay," Steve returned. There was no cockiness in his voice, just self-assurance.

"It takes a long time to become a jockey," Alec said.

"Not in my case," Steve answered.

Alec looked at him in surprise, but the youth had turned to the Black, who was still watching him.

"It's almost as if he knows you," Alec said. "He doesn't usually act this way with strangers."

"It's the first time I've seen him except on television," Steve said.

"He has a keener sense of smell than most horses," Alec said. "Maybe it's something on you."

Steve Duncan laughed, completely relaxed for the first time. "Maybe so. I got all spit-and-polished to come out here. It could be the after-shave lotion."

"It could be," Alec said, "but it isn't. It's something else."

The Black was cool and collected, but there was no doubt he had picked up the faintest whiff of a familiar scent from Steve Duncan. What it was, was anybody's guess.

"It your horse a stallion?" Alec asked.

"Very much so," Steve answered.

The Black's foretop fell in his eyes and he tossed his head to get rid of it. He pulled on the lead shank, balking a little when Alec tried to straighten him out.

"Is he sound?" Steve asked.

"He's doing fine," Alec said. "I give him fourteen to sixteen quarts of oats a day and his feed tub is as shiny as a new quarter when he's finished."

"I mean in the head?"

"He's sound in the head, too," Alec answered, smiling a little, and wondering what had prompted such a question.

"Do you ever trust him to anyone else?" Steve asked.

"Seldom. You can't push him at all. He'll strike back every time."

"It must be rough working around him," Steve said.

"No, we just have to be a little careful. Usually, it's about little things, like a coarse brush. He hates it. Sometimes he strikes out when I'm even using a fine brush, but the good thing about it is that he doesn't aim any more. He just lets you know he doesn't like it."

Alec rubbed his right knee and added, "He caught me this morning but not intentionally. He was just playing and, luckily, he didn't hit me square or he would have broken the cap."

Steve said, "He must have some disposition . . . like a bull."

"He's rugged and in good health, if that's what you mean."

"I guess you could race him anywhere," Steve replied. "I mean *any* track in the country would make room for him."

"We go where the racing suits him," Alec admitted. "But you're right. All we've got to do is pick up a phone and tell them we're coming. We don't have any trouble getting stall space, if that's what you mean."

"It's tough getting a stall here, isn't it?"

"It's not easy," Alec said, studying the boy's face, for he knew they were slowly getting around to the purpose of his visit. "Hialeah is the only major racetrack in the East operating during January and February. All the big stables that have stock to race are here. It makes for a very busy place."

Steve Duncan met Alec's close scrutiny without flinching. He tried to smile but it was not a success. Finally, he said, "My horse could win here, if I could get stall space. I'm sure of it."

For a few minutes Alec said nothing. He'd met lots of other fellows who wanted to become jockeys. But this was the first time one had ever come to him with a horse to race. He couldn't laugh it off as Henry had done. Certainly not now, with Steve Duncan's thin, sharp and very determined face only inches away from his.

"It's best not to get too high on *any* horse," Alec said. "I tell myself that all the time, even with the Black. There's always a terrific sense of disappointment when you go overboard and the horse doesn't pan out."

"I feel pretty good about my horse," Steve said.

"I'm sure you do," Alec answered, "but winning a race at Hialeah is something else again."

"He can beat anything here, even yours."

Alec turned away. The whole thing was becoming ridiculous. Perhaps Henry had been right. He'd have done better to keep away from this wild-eyed Steve Duncan.

"Okay," he said finally. "So you've got a fast horse. What makes you think you can ride him in a race? It takes years of experience."

Steve Duncan's dark eyes brightened. "I read a story in the paper the other day about an eleven-year-old kid riding his first race in England."

"I read something in the paper the other day, too," Alec said. "I read that 4-H Clubs all over the country are developing riding and horsemanship as part of their activities. That's good. Kids will learn to ride all the better for it, and be better off physically and mentally."

"You're being a wise guy," Steve Duncan said angrily.

"No, not at all. I'm only trying to say that you shouldn't look forward to becoming a jockey overnight. It takes time and patience. Two or three years, maybe, of hard work and long hours."

Steve laughed. "I don't think there's much difference in riders," he said, "even race-riders. Get on the best horse and you're the best rider. It's as simple as that."

"It isn't," Alec said. "Even the best horse can lose races through bad riding. The only way to learn good riding is to start from the bottom. You learn first how a racing stable operates. You groom. You walk hots. You ride exercise ponies and learn the rules of racing. Then, if you've proven to be able, you gallop and breeze horses. You take blackboard drills. You study patrol movies. You learn the duties of the stewards, the placing judges, the patrol judges and last, but not least, the starters. You—"

"You're kidding," Steve interrupted. "You don't need all that, not if you're on the right horse at the right time. You ought to know that. You of all people. You had nothing but *him* when you started. That's why I'm here."

Alec held the other's eyes. *"Nothing but him,"* Steve had said. Nothing but the Black and a mutual love and understanding for each other. Steve Duncan was right. He'd had no thick calluses on his hands in those days.

"But I had Henry Dailey as a friend and trainer," he said finally. "Without him, I doubt very much that I would have raced the Black."

"I know that," Steve Duncan said surprisingly. "That's why I came to you. I hoped you'd help me as you were helped."

Alec said nothing, but he knew he could no longer look upon Steve Duncan's request as anything but the deadly serious matter it was. His visitor had struck home.

Steve Duncan went on, confident that Alec was listening now to every word he had to say. "I know you meant what you said about learning all those things having to do with racing, and taking two or three years to do it. But I don't want to be a professional rider, Alec. I just need money now, lots of it. The only way I can get it is to race my horse."

"How much money?" Alec asked, and he was surprised at the casualness of his voice. "And what for?" Steve Duncan would not want the money for anything foolish. Of that Alec was convinced now. There was no doubt Steve knew what he was after, and that he had a plan to get it.

"I need sixty-five thousand dollars to buy an island," Steve answered. It was said the same way most people would have talked about earning money for a home or food or any of the basic necessities of life.

"An island," Alec repeated, his voice as matter-of-fact as Steve's. Two guys talking. That was the way it could go sometimes. "You going to live there?"

"No, but my horse does."

"Oh," Alec said, as if Steve had explained everything. "I thought you might have won your racehorse in a contest or something. You know there's a pipe tobacco company that gives away two racehorses every year just for naming them."

"I didn't get Flame that way," Steve answered. "You know it's funny about those contests," he went on seriously. "For years I tried to win a horse that way. But it was always women who won the contests."

"Housewives," Alec added, as serious as Steve. "I don't understand it either."

The Black moved around them in a tight circle and their gazes turned to him.

"Is your island nearby?" Alec asked Steve.

"No, it's way down in the Caribbean Sea." Steve

hesitated, his eyes wavering a moment, then meeting Alec's again. "It's in the Windward group of the Lower Antilles."

"We were down that way a few months ago," Alec said. "Not by choice. We ran into Daisy."

"The hurricane. Yeah, I know. I read about your plane having to ditch. It's a wonder—"

"I know," Alec said, cutting him off. "It is. But we're here." He didn't want to discuss that episode in his life.

"You wouldn't have seen my island," Steve said. "It's not much."

"Is that why you want to buy it?"

"That's why I *can* buy it," Steve said. "It's a British possession and uninhabited. Her Majesty's government will sell it for sixty-five thousand dollars."

"You're sure?"

"We checked and that's what we learned."

"*We?*" Alec repeated. "*Your parents?*"

"No, my friend Pitch. He's old. I mean older than us. Maybe he's like your friend Henry, except different."

"How different?"

"He's no trainer or even a horseman. He's an amateur archaeologist and historian."

"Oh," Alec said.

"That's why he's interested in the island," Steve explained further.

"Is he there now with your horse?"

"He's with my horse, but not there."

Alec started to say "Oh" again but changed his mind and kept still. It was better if he didn't give Steve the impression that he understood when he didn't. One step at a time.

"Then your horse and Pitch are here? I mean in Miami?"

"No, they're in Nassau over in the Bahamas."

"*Oh*" slipped out before Alec could check it. He went on, "They're as good as here, then. Just a few hours away."

"I can bring Flame to Hialeah, if you'll help me."

"How?" Alec heard himself ask quite seriously.

"Speak to the racing secretary. Try to get me stall space. It would take just one big race for me to win all the money I need."

The Black started around them in another tight circle. Alec, who felt he couldn't be made any dizzier than he was, stayed with him this time instead of giving him enough shank to go around alone. This Steve Duncan was fantastic in his requests. The Black kept circling.

"That's a big order," Alec said finally. "I wouldn't have a chance of doing what you ask. The secretary would never go for my story of a phantom horse that was so fast he could . . . well, go as fast as you say yours can go."

Steve's black eyes flashed fire again. "He's no phantom horse," he said.

"I'm sure he isn't," Alec said quietly. "Not to you, but he would be to the racing secretary. Occasionally," he went on, "I've heard of some horse like yours being given permission to enter the United States for 'racing purposes only.' But always he's won some race to make it worthwhile for a racing secretary to *want* him at his track."

Alec studied Steve's thin, drawn face, waiting for him to say his horse had won something that would make him wanted at Hialeah. But his visitor remained silent, as if torn between conflicting emotions.

Alec felt his sympathy for Steve Duncan getting out of hand, almost to the point of his *having* to do something for him. "Since you have Flame in Nassau, why not race him there?" he suggested. "If he's as good as you say he is, he'll win in such fast time people over here will certainly become aware of him. Then we'll have something to work with."

"We?" Steve repeated. "You'll help me, then?"

"If you do as I say and race him in Nassau," Alec promised. "We can go on from there, depending upon how you make out."

"I'll do it!" Steve Duncan said. His voice was so shrill that it startled the Black, who took two jumps and came to a stop only when Alec had been pulled off his feet and lay on the ground.

Reaching for Alec's hand, Steve helped him up. "That's all I need. I'll be back soon, Alec . . . you'll see." He turned and fled down the shed row, a skinny, running figure in a black suit.

Alec watched him go. *You'll need lots more than my help*, he thought. But whether or not Flame raced successfully in Nassau, Alec felt certain he had not seen the last of Steve Duncan. Strangely enough, he was glad. It was good to be shaken up once in a while, to be made to realize how it had been for him, too, at the beginning. And he'd been shook, plenty.

Misty Morning

3

The next morning Alec's alarm clock went off at five minutes to five, giving him the usual five minutes to convince himself it was time to get up. He had no set deadline to meet, for Henry seldom sent the Black out on the track before eight o'clock in the morning. There was a time when Henry had made a daybreak gallop a must, but such was not the case in Florida. Henry was slowing up.

With seven hours of sleep behind him, Alec got out of bed. There was a little chill to the morning air, just enough to be invigorating without any need for a warming fire. Such mornings made winter racing in Florida most attractive. Later on, he'd listen to the radio and find out how cold it was up north.

After turning on the light, Alec dressed slowly. Outside the barn he heard the muffled snorts and neighs of horses and the mutterings of caretakers. Many horses had been fed as early as three-thirty and very shortly, with the rising of the sun, they would be on their way to the track.

The Black was behind the closed doors of his stall, resting and undisturbed by the area's predawn activities. Alec knew that his horse adjusted well to any schedule set for him. Perhaps he even enjoyed these extra hours of luxury as much as Alec himself did.

Henry was in his motel just a few blocks away, still asleep. It was his old friend's right, Alec conceded, although there were times when he wished he could have changed places with Henry. He rubbed the sleep out of his eyes and had trouble finding his clothes.

Henry wasn't a true ractracker any more, Alec decided as he dressed. These days he ate a big breakfast at his motel before going to the track. A year ago Henry would have had only a cup of coffee, saving his bacon and eggs and toast until about ten o'clock, when their morning work was finished.

Alec left the tack room, still sleepy, and not bothering to identify any of the shadowy figures moving about the area. He was greeted by a loud snort as he opened the Black's stall door and turned on the light. Once inside, his eyes moved quickly to the corner rack, noting that there was hay left from the night before. He emptied and washed the water bucket, then refilled it. He set in the morning feed and left the Black alone to eat.

The stallion's morning meal was the lightest of the day, consisting only of dry oats. Henry had special food and mineral additives which were included in all other meals. Alec didn't know if they helped the Black or not. They certainly could do no harm. Of course they helped Henry, who was taking the same wheat-germ oil and blood-liver tonic, high in iron, that he was giving the Black. Henry was trying all kinds of tonics these days. Let anyone make a suggestion about

the ways and means to better health and he'd be the
first to try it.

Alec washed up and then went to the track kitchen
for a cup of coffee. He didn't linger over it or spend
any time with the other men who were there, for he
had a lot of work to do before Henry arrived.

Night was gradually fading, giving way to shadowy
dawn as he walked back to the barn. Figures in the
area were becoming clearer and some of the boys were
already riding toward the track. Alec mucked out the
Black's stall and rebedded it, saving whatever straw he
could. It was expensive in Florida, just as good hay
was. He talked to the Black as he worked and noted
that his feed tub was clean, always a wonderful sign.
The Black would have time to digest his oats before
going out on the track.

After finishing his work in the stall Alec began
grooming the Black. No one else could do this job, not
even Henry. It made for a long day but there was no
alternative. Henry insisted that a good groom was
equal in value to a good horse. It was impossible to
have one without the other.

The Black stood still as Alec went over him with soft
rub-rags and soft brushes. Finally, there were only the
steel-shod feet to clean. When that was done Alec
said, "I'm glad you're not playing tricks any more. See
that you act this way on the track. My knee is still
bruised from the kick you gave me yesterday."

When Alec left the stall and stepped outside he
found that a light breeze was blowing. There was mist,
too, but that would dissipate with the rising sun. It
was a time of day that he especially liked. There was

no other hour like it; he felt sorry for everybody who was still in bed and asleep.

He went into the tack room and changed his sneakers for boots. Then, picking up his riding helmet, he fitted a freshly washed black-and-white silk cap over the tough fiber headpiece. He punched his fist into the soft and thick sponge-rubber lining. It made sense that such a protective hat was part of a jockey's required equipment. Most people had no idea what riding into the first turn was like. Steel-shod hoofs made a pretty sound on a race track but not on a guy's head. Making racehorses go was a tough, hazardous business for men as well as boys. Their careers were relatively short and not many of them ever became rich.

The sun was up when Henry arrived. He loitered outside where it shone brightly down on him, as if he needed warmth in his old bones. Alec glanced impatiently toward the track. The sun was shining there, too, and he was anxious to ride. The cool air acted as a tonic for him.

"You're late," he told Henry. "Let's get going."

Henry blinked in the bright sunlight but did not move. He seemed to be listening to the singing of the birds in the lush greenery nearby. Finally, his eyes focused on Alec.

"Just think," he said. "It's near zero in New York again today."

Alec started up the shed row, hoping Henry would follow. He went into the Black's stall but came right out again when Henry didn't join him. The old trainer was across the way, visiting a litter of stable kittens

that had been born a few days before. Shrugging his
shoulders, Alec thought resignedly, what was his big
rush anyway? They had all morning, and patience was
the secret to success in this business, as perhaps in any
business.

He returned to the Black. Maybe they should have
brought old Napoleon along. The gray gelding was the
Black's mascot. Almost every good horse had a mascot
or pet of some kind, like the kittens across the way.
Elsewhere in the area were ponies, donkeys, goats,
monkeys and dogs. Most stable mascots were useful
for they soothed temperamental horses or acted as
watchdogs; others were only decorative or thought to
bring good luck. A billy goat, not a nanny goat, was
supposed to ward off disease in a barn. Birds, except
for chickens and ducks, were supposed to be bad luck
and avoided. Monkeys and roosters usually thought
they were jockeys, for they were forever perched on
the backs of their protégés.

Alec slipped on the Black's bridle, then the light
saddle, his strong, calloused hands gentle on the big
horse. Outside, he remarked, "He's on his toes this
morning, Henry."

"Ain't he always?" the old trainer said, his eyes on
the Black. They had a big and handsome hunk of
horseflesh. He had put on weight during the past year
but had not lost his racing trim. "He'll look good on
TV again this year," he added seriously. There was no
doubt that television had done much to endow the
Black with more appeal and grandeur than any horse
since Pegasus. It was one of those things that had
changed with the times. In the old days one had to see

a great horse in the flesh to appreciate him. Not any more.

The Black shifted quickly when Henry boosted Alec into the saddle, but the old trainer held the lead shank tightly while Alec took up his reins and got set. Then they started down the row, the gazes of all the men in the area following them.

Alec glanced at the tall Australian pines just beyond. The rays of the morning sun were filtering their way through; it was still a little misty but beginning to clear.

A filly went along the path at a slow jog, her rider standing in his stirrup irons and talking to her. The Black jumped after them and Alec said, "Easy, mister. Easy."

"There goes a nervous, fidgety filly," Henry pointed out. "I wouldn't have her in my stable."

"She's young," Alec said. "She'll settle down." He knotted the reins, keeping his mind on his own horse. The Black was getting stronger as he got older.

"Perhaps so," Henry answered, his eyes still on the filly. "But it's always better to be surprised then disappointed. It takes a lot of time with the good ones."

"Sure, Henry," Alec said. He knew what his friend meant. Take all the time in the world so nothing would ever come to an end. Henry would rust away if he found himself without a horse to train, and the Black was the biggest one he'd had.

The filly up ahead went into a spin, rearing and almost spilling her rider.

"She's green and hard to handle," Henry said. "She

raced only twice last year. That's Manizales up on her."

"I know," Alec said, having recognized the little Puerto Rican from the dark turtleneck sweater and scarlet headpiece he always wore. "She won't get rid of Manny."

"No, she won't. He's one jock who didn't come here to go fishing or get away from cold weather."

"I've been watching him race," Alec said. "He's a go-for-broke rider every time."

"He's hungry," Henry said, "and that makes him reckless. It also makes him unpopular with other jockeys as well as the stewards."

"It should," Alec said. "He almost put Charley Hancox in the infield yesterday. I don't know how he got away with not being suspended."

"He's a smart rider as well as a rough one," Henry said. "He makes it difficult for anyone to claim a foul."

Alec shrugged his shoulders. "He sure does everything at a quick pace. I guess he wants to succeed in the United States in a hurry."

"He's not alone," Henry said. "There are plenty of others from the islands who think they can get rich quick at Hialeah."

Alec found himself thinking of Steve Duncan's visit the day before. He had told Henry last evening that Steve had arrived but not about his need for so much money or the reason for it. Henry wouldn't have believed him anyway.

"But I'll say this for them," Henry continued, his gaze following Manizales. "They're out galloping horses every morning. They work a lot harder than most of our more popular jockeys. That's why a good many trainers are using them in the afternoons as well."

They arrived at the gap in the fence, and many friends leaning on the rail turned to greet them.

"Morning, boys," one trainer called; his eyes were not on Alec and Henry but on the Black.

The morning sun made the infield grass look yellowish-green. Spindly-legged, pink-coated flamingos inhabited the centerfield lake and a few were flying above, their wings catching the sun's rays as they soared over the pines that lined the backstretch. But most of the four hundred birds were still asleep, and one saw them only as shadowy shapes along the edges of the lake.

Henry held the Black steady, seemingly in no hurry to turn him loose and enjoying the attention they were getting. The tight little group along the rail broke up, the men coming toward them. There was friendly banter, some of it of a joking sort, most of it serious. Over it all was the muffled sound of steel-shod hoofs passing by on the track.

"He looks awfully good," one friend said.

"He should," Henry answered. "I got to keep training him or he'll fill up on me."

"What's he weigh now, about eleven hundred?"

"I'd guess about that," Henry said. "Actually, I'm taking it easy with him. I figure I could do more harm overworking him than anything else."

"You ought to know." The other laughed. "You've had him long enough. A nice way to make a living, Henry."

"Yeah, it is easier to make a living with a horse you know an' understand," Henry admitted.

"At least it gets you south for the winter. Sixteen days below freezing up north. That ain't for me any more." The man studied the Black. "He sure looks the part of a champion, Henry. I guess he's enjoying all the publicity he's been getting, huh?"

"Maybe so. Sometimes I think he can read."

"I heard you been sneaking in some workouts at three o'clock in the morning."

Henry chuckled. "Don't you believe it. I quit doin' that some years ago. I had a horse get lost in the darkness and fall in the centerfield lake."

A veteran clocker turned from the rail after having clicked his stopwatch on a working horse. "You still got to show us he's as great as he was last year, Henry," he said. "We're influenced only by this." He lifted the watch.

"We're not out to prove anything to you, George," Henry said. "We're just aimin' to win races."

"There are some tough ones coming up."

"We're not lookin' for tough spots for him. We're tryin' to make it as fair for him as we can."

"It looks to me," someone said, "that he just eats an' sleeps an' maintains banker's hours. You're takin' it awfully easy with him these mornings."

Henry smiled. "Like I said, Tom. I don't like to rush a big horse. But maybe we *will* go scouting around for a race any day now."

"That'll please the management," a reporter said, smiling. "Anytime the Black races new attendance records are set. The more 'name' horses around here, the better Hialeah likes it."

Henry said with attempted modesty, "It's true they've been after me to start him. The Black's got quite a public following."

"That's putting it lightly," the reporter said. "You know as well as I do that he can set these turnstiles clicking like no other horse in the country. He has crowd-appeal, like Babe Ruth had in baseball. He's got all the glamour and appeal."

"Glamour and appeal nothin'," a noted trainer interrupted. "He's just a great big clown an' that's why they come to see him race. There's no telling what he might do. He might stay in front or come from behind or even loaf at times. You never know, like I say, and that's what makes him so popular."

Alec smiled. Everybody thought they knew everything about his horse. Actually, nobody but himself was aware of what went on out there.

Henry said, "The last thing I'd do would be to ruin his great record for a little money or to please the track management. He won't race before he's ready to go."

"You're on a day-to-day basis with him then," the reporter said, making a note in his book.

"You might call it that," Henry answered. "His racing depends pretty much on his response to training."

"Then he looks like he's ready to go now," the reporter said.

"No, he's just a hardy horse, that's all," Henry said. "Black horses usually are hardier than others for some reason." He smiled. "They're also harder to keep clean. Sweat just seems to stick to them. You have no idea how hard Alec rubs him to get him to look like this."

The clocker with the lined, intent face smiled for the first time. "I heard Alec uses only a silk handkerchief," he said. "You know, to sort of pacify him."

"Just another fable," Henry said, smiling back.

The reporter asked, "Will you say for publication that he's a better horse now than he was last year?"

Henry didn't waver for an instant. "There are a lot of 'ifs' but I honestly think so," he said.

A group of six horses went by in a run, their riders all wearing the red-and-blue jackets from the same stable. Everybody on the rail turned to watch the mock race until the set had flashed under the finish line.

"Nice thing about a big outfit is that they can stage a conditioning race any morning they please," a trainer said. "It gives the horses the competition they need. It's worth five mornings, working alone."

A single horse came around the far turn and their gazes turned now to Manizales riding his fiery filly.

"She has a habit of galloping with her head low," the veteran clocker said, "especially when Manny digs into her and arouses all her fighting spirit."

"It makes her look smaller than she actually is," Henry said. "But you're right . . . she has a great heart."

The filly swept by with Manizales rocking in his saddle, urging her on. She was being blown out for a race the next day, her first of the year.

Another horse rounded the far turn, coming down over the turf course on the other side of the inner rail.

He was a walloper in size, but his strides were short despite the urging of his rider.

"That's Bolero, up from the Argentine," the clocker said. "He's turf champion of South America, but you'd never know it from his works. I've been watching him for two weeks now and he's a complete bust in the morning. He's either too lazy or too smart, or perhaps a little bit of both. In any case, they have to do everything short of pushing him around the track to get him to break out of a slow walk."

Henry watched the big horse as he came closer, noting the wonderful leverage of his hind legs even at such a slow gait. It indicated enormous propulsion whenever Bolero *did* decide to run. The rest of him, too, gave the impression of power. He was not a showy horse, his head being too large and his nose Roman, curved and protruding. He looked very plain except for the massive, muscular neck and the heavy but well-laid shoulders. His limbs were sturdy and in proportion to his great size. Watching him go by, Henry knew that this horse would give trouble to others at Hialeah, including the Black, whenever he decided to race.

Turning to Alec, Henry said, "Take the Black over the grass course this morning. Go a mile in one forty-six or one forty-seven, that's all I want. Ease up for another furlong and then bring him back."

Alec nodded, knowing full well he had a difficult task before him. The Black was anxious to run a little. He wouldn't like being held down to the slow time Henry had ordered. It didn't matter that the workout would be over the turf course. The Black's running action was high, which meant he would stride well over the grass rather than through it. Horses with low action usually had more trouble on turf courses, being stopped to some extent by having to cut through the grass.

Henry released the Black, and Alec rode him onto the track, standing in his stirrups while going past the long stands. Two fast working horses swept by close to the inner rail. Directly behind them another horse followed, his face being whipped by flying sand. The trailing horse didn't like it and was trying to pull to one side. His rider kept him directly behind the leaders and Alec knew he was being subjected to the stinging dirt on purpose. A lot of good horses would refuse to race under such conditions. The Black was not one of them. Alec had brought him back from winning races with his eyes almost completely closed by grit.

Reaching the infield gate, Alec rode onto the grass. The Black responded quickly to the soft cushion, his strides lengthening as he fought the restraining hold on his mouth.

"Easy," Alec said, still standing in his irons.

The Black's strides shortened. There had been a time when he resented rating but now he was settling down with maturity. Most of the time he would do as Alec wanted. Most of the time, but not always.

A number of flamingos rose from the other side of the hedge as Alec turned the Black loose. He saw their wings soar overhead but they were gone quickly. He leaned forward, close to the Black's neck.

The long strides came fast. The thing about his

horse, Alec thought, was that he could get started so quickly you had to be ready immediately or he'd leave you behind. His strides were at least five feet longer than any other horse's, which meant he'd cover more ground without taking more strides than another horse running alongside.

Alec loosened his hold on the reins. There must be no strain on the Black's mouth while the horse settled into his far-reaching, level run. He wanted the Black's head *out*, not up and fighting him. He sat there quietly, doing nothing more than steering, if that. The Black kept close to the inner hedge and it was hard for Alec to tell how fast he was going over the grass once he hit full stride. Also, there was little bouncing around on his back, for the Black remained almost in a horizontal position when he went after speed, floating along without any jar to his rider whatsoever.

Entering the backstretch, Alec felt they were going at just about the fractions Henry had ordered. But he couldn't be sure, with the Black running so easily. When the half-mile pole whipped by, Alec decided he had better take hold a little more.

But the Black was full of run and wouldn't ease up for Alec. He went into the far turn, his speed unchecked and changing leads perfectly. Alec had hoped for a bit of clumsiness during the change, a momentary loss of action which would have given him a chance to ease up the Black. That didn't happen. His horse leaned into the final bend and entered the upper stretch still in high gear.

Alec couldn't be sure what speed they were making, but he was afraid it wasn't what Henry had ordered.

Again he tried to slow down the Black. They whipped by the group watching them. He thought he saw Henry swinging his straw hat at him, but he couldn't be sure of that, either.

Sometimes, he told himself, it just wasn't possible to work a horse as a trainer had ordered. Sometimes everything went wrong from the very beginning. This seemed to be one of those mornings. The Black had turned on a lot of speed before he had been fully aware of it.

Alec glanced at the mile pole that seemed to be coming rapidly toward them. For all he knew they were going the distance in the time Henry had ordered. Maybe they'd be just a tick off the 1:46 or 1:47 Henry had wanted.

The Black finished the mile still floating along with his ears pricked. He responded to Alec's hands soon after crossing the finish line, as if he knew he had completed the course.

Alec let him go another furlong before turning him around. He saw Henry walking toward them, brushing off his clothes as if he had fallen in the dirt. The straw hat was in his hand, and Alec recalled the glimpse he'd had of Henry waving it as they had swept past.

Henry took hold of the Black's bridle without a word and led the horse off the track, past the men huddled together who were watching them. "You didn't have to do it," he said angrily to Alec when they were on their way back to the barn.

"Do what?"

"Do one thirty-seven for the mile, a whole ten

seconds faster than I told you to go."

"I had no idea."

"You should!" Henry bellowed. "You're supposed to be a top jockey. You're supposed to be able to do more than just sit there."

"I'm sorry."

The old man grunted fiercely. He hadn't looked at Alec since he had taken hold of the Black's bridle. Nor did he do so now. Back at the barn he removed his straw hat and began to wash down the Black in angry silence.

Alec tried again. "I know it was my fault."

"It was," Henry said.

"I really kept a hold on him all the time."

"Just enough to let him know you were up there, that's all," the old man said. "You just let him set his own pace, figuring he'd get the job done all by himself, I suppose."

"He likes to go his own way," Alec said sheepishly. "He doesn't like to have me take too much hold."

"That's always a good excuse for poor riding and judgment," Henry said. "I don't go for it. Never did. No horse should be allowed to run a race as *he* sees it."

"But I worked at it," Alec said in his own defense. "He had me puffing."

Henry snorted. "It was just a gallop for you. I watched you every second with the glasses."

"Maybe it was the grass that made it seem he was going slower than he was," Alec suggested lamely. "He liked it better than I thought he would."

Henry picked up the left forefoot, examining it closely.

"At least," Alec went on hurriedly, "this work ought to prove to you that he's sound enough to race."

Henry put down the foot, and continued washing down the muscular black horse.

"You were worried about his foot, Henry," Alec tried again. "So now you ought to feel lots better than you did."

The Black was nippy and full of life. The fast workout had done him a world of good.

Henry said, "It was the first time you ever did anything as bad as that to me, Alec."

"It wasn't intentional," Alec persisted.

"You just sat there," the old man repeated.

"I never took him over a grass course before," Alec said. "I didn't know. He seemed to be moving so effortlessly."

"He was," Henry said. "But you still should have known how fast he was going. If you can't rate him, no one can, and we might as well go home. I tell you again that no horse can win races running them *his* way. He needs guidance, and that means *rating* by his rider. Maybe you're forgetting some of the things you had to learn the hard way. Maybe it's time we started doing our homework again."

"If you say so, Henry," Alec said quietly, knowing now what was ahead of him. There would be lessons on riding tactics every night along with blackboard drills. There would be patrol movies to review and races to watch. It might turn out to be a long, hard winter after all.

The Roll
of Thunder...

4

The Associated Press sent the following story to its member newspapers throughout the United States:

The Black, looking stronger and possibly better than ever, was given his first mile speed drill over Hialeah's soft turf course this morning in preparation for his defense of the Handicap Championship Crown. The mighty stallion handled the grass with ease, demonstrating that any footing suits him. His fractions were 23-4/5ths for the first quarter, :47 for the half mile, 1:11 for three-quarters, and the mile in 1:37. Going handily, he was eased out another eighth in 1:51.

Observers were impressed with the excellent progress the champion has made. He cooled out perfectly with no sign of heat or swelling in the injured leg that has kept him sidelined for almost a year.

Henry Dailey would not commit himself as to the Black's first race at Hialeah. "He's too good a horse to make any definite statement about it," the veteran trainer said, "but he won't run until he's completely ready. I can't make that too plain. We won't start him one second too early." It is believed, however, that Dailey is pointing the Black for the rich Hialeah Turf Cup and the Widener Handicap. The champion is sure to carry top weight in both events, based on today's sterling performance.

The news story added fuel to Henry's anger, and he lost no time in taking it out on Alec. "In my day, the trainer was the boss. A rider did what he said or he gave him a good boot and sent him on his way."

"It's not always that easy to follow orders," Alec said.

"It is if you work at it," Henry said. "Most of you fellows got it too easy today. That's why riders like Manizales are winning so many races here. They're willing to work hard at their profession."

"That's not all there is to it," Alec said. "Manny was no Grade B rider in Puerto Rico but the best in his country. So were most of the South Americans who are riding here. Send our best riders down there and they'll do as well."

"Not if they don't work hard," Henry said adamantly.

"I work hard," Alec said, losing his patience and becoming defiant for the first time. "Just because I didn't rate him right this morning is no reason—"

"You slip up on one thing and you'll start doing lots of other things wrong," Henry interrupted. "I'm going to stop you right now. There are a lot of things I'm going to check you out on."

Alec's homework began that evening. While Henry threw questions at him, he answered as best he could. They covered a great deal in that first session—rating a horse and race strategy, as well as all the tricks Henry had ever taught him as to how to protect himself. The sessions would go on indefinitely, Alec knew, whenever time was available. Henry would try Alec's patience and never give him a free moment.

When he finally went to bed that night, Alec welcomed the sudden cloudburst that hammered the roof with staccatolike intensity. Perhaps the driving downpour would keep up all night and well into the next morning. If so, Henry would sleep late. Henry's blood had thinned out, or so he said, and his bones were brittle. He couldn't take dampness and rain any more. He had tried to stand it once or twice during the past year but had finally given up. He had gone to bed and stayed there.

When the alarm clock sounded the next morning, Alec woke up to find that summer was over. The temperature was in the low fifties, and there was a cold dampness that seemed to penetrate his bones. When he went outside, he saw that low and ominous clouds hung overhead. Alec went about his work, knowing that Henry wouldn't appear until late in the morning, if at all, and that he and the Black were in for a well-earned rest.

The heavy clouds delayed the approach of dawn and a high wind whipped about the stable area. Horses were being fed and cared for, but few, if any, would appear for exercise unless weather conditions im-

proved. As the hours went by, Alec, wearing long
rubber pants and a heavy sweater, continued working
by himself. This wasn't exactly his kind of weather
either, although he remained grateful for the rest it
afforded him.

The rain was still falling steadily when Henry
arrived close to noon. He was blue with cold, despite
the fact that he was wearing an overcoat. It had been
borrowed and was much too large for him, but at least
it provided some warmth. "I went back to bed," he
said. "I wouldn't want to take him out in this."

Alec nodded. He could have said that mud and cold
had never been a problem to the Black, but he didn't.
He, too, was tired of getting mud in his face, and that
was what would have happened on the track this
morning, even at a slow gallop.

"This is enough to drive a guy back up north,"
Henry complained.

The blustery wind whipped through the area with
tornadolike force and overhead a long streak of
lightning shattered the heavens.

"It can't make up its mind whether to snow or
become a tropical storm," Alec said. "Either way it's
going to cut the attendance figures this afternoon."

"We'll be in the stands," Henry said. "You and I got
work to do."

"I figured that," Alec replied glumly. "Or you
would have stayed in bed."

There were other places he'd rather be than in
Hialeah's stands that afternoon. But as Henry had said
many times last night, *he* was the boss. You did what

he said or *he* gave you a boot. These were old, old times, all over again.

By post time for the first race Alec was sitting in the stands with Henry, shivering and uncomfortable along with some five thousand other die-hard fans. The spindly-legged flamingos in centerfield looked naked and very cold. If their wings had not been pinioned to prevent long-distance flying, Alec was certain the whole flock of four hundred birds would have taken off for their island homes to the south.

Rain continued to fall steadily and the long brown stretch past the half-filled stands was deep in slop. The track management was doing its best to brighten up the day. The band, well protected beneath the roof of the grandstand, was giving forth with loud groans and oom-pahs from its instruments for an afternoon of music. Its maestro must have been flogging the musicians to get them to play "Oh, What a Beautiful Morning" on such a day.

The gondolier, poling his authentic Venetian gondola on the infield lake, was active too despite the weather. He maneuvered his boat around the edges of the lagoon, apparently trying to arouse the half-frozen flamingos. Few if any fans watched him or cared what went on in centerfield. It was no day for a show or carnival. There were no tourists who needed to be entertained by birds, boats or a band. Those in the stands had come only to watch the best horseflesh of the year.

"It's surprising there are so many here on a day like

this," Alec commented.

Henry nodded in agreement and mumbled that perhaps most of them were owners, for in this jet age it was possible for a man to leave New York or Chicago in the morning and get to Hialeah in time to watch his horse race. He could even return home in time for dinner. While he was speaking, Henry's teeth were chattering with cold.

An assistant starter walked across the track, lifting his rubber-booted legs heavily out of the mud with each stride.

Alec said, "It won't be long before they'll be using a synthetic strip over a track like this. Remember the one they had under the starting gate at Saratoga last year? The only trouble was that it didn't go all the way around to the finish."

"It's too expensive," Henry muttered.

"But so are good horses," Alec answered. "And many are badly hurt on a track like this."

"To say nothing of their riders," Henry added, looking at Alec.

"Sure," the youth agreed. "I don't see any reason why a synthetic track would be too expensive when you consider the benefits. The resin strip is only an inch thick and could be laid in sections. When it was not in use it could be rolled and put in centerfield."

Henry nodded thoughtfully. "Sure, we might see it one of these days. It might not be any more expensive than some of the carnival acts they put on in center-field." He paused to listen to the imperative bugle call of "Boots and Saddles" as it came rattling out of the amplifiers, then added, "I've seen a lot of good horses fall . . . then have to be destroyed . . . because of such going as this."

The first race of the afternoon was for three-year-olds and up over a distance of one mile. Out of the tunnel which led from the paddock area to the track came a red-coated marshall, followed by the field of eight horses. Alec watched them emerge, thinking of other afternoons when he had seen young horses with great speed and heart seek their place in the sun before the eyes of a clamoring crowd. Today there was no sun, nor was there a crowd or fanfare. The stands were quiet as the horses stepped onto the Hialeah track beneath the black, ominous sky.

"I want you to watch Manizales closely in this one," Henry said. "Maybe you'll learn something."

The horse Manizales was riding was the green and fractious filly he had blown out the day before. Watching her, Alec could sense that she was very scared.

"She doesn't like the mud," he said quietly. "She runs hard, really digs in. A firm track is better suited for her."

"Nothing suits her, not yet," Henry said. "That's why I want you to watch how Manny handles her. She's a rank outsider in this field. All the others are scared of her, including the trainers. I don't mean they're scared of her speed, just her shenanigans."

"Today of all days," Alec said.

"It depends on how you look at it," Henry said. "In her last start as a two-year-old she shied at a shadow and bolted into the rail. She don't need no shadow roll

THE ROLL OF THUNDER . . .   55

on a day like this. Maybe she'll do just fine."

"Maybe," Alec repeated, "but I doubt it."

"Anyhow, they can't keep her from starting today.
But if she gets out of control in this race, she might be
barred hereafter."

"That might be too late," Alec said, watching the
filly trying to unseat Manizales during the post
parade.

"With all her nervousness, she's slow at the break,"
Henry said. "She hesitates and lets the others get
away from her. Watch Manny in the gate. He hasn't
been able to do much with her."

Alec smiled. "You mean you want me to learn from
his mistakes as well as my own," he said flatly.

"It's possible," Henry shot back. "It's one thing to
profit from mistakes and something else again to profit
from instruction. You can do both if you put your mind
to it."

"My mind's put to it," Alec said, his eyes on the
sucking mass of mud that stretched from rail to rail.
The rain started coming down harder and the wind
rose almost to gale force. He wondered how the
jockeys were able to stay in their saddles.

"Manny might be too aggressive," Henry said, "but
he never holds a grudge when he's been set down for a
few days by an official. He takes his punishment like a
man and comes back smiling." Henry glanced at Alec
to see if the boy was listening to him.

Alec said, "You mean that I don't."

"I didn't say that."

"No, but you meant it," Alec returned. "Okay,
Henry, I'm taking it and smiling."

Henry turned his gaze back to the horses. "I don't want to act like any Dutch uncle."

"You're not."

"It's just that maybe I see a lot of things that you miss. It's only natural. It's been my job for a long time. And I find an awful lot of sacks riding horses these days, jocks who should be anywhere but out there."

"You're not including Manizales?"

"No, all he needs to do is to master his fiery temper during the running of a race. Most of the rest he's got. His reflexes are quick and he's able to make split-second decisions so long as he doesn't get mad. He knows how to save ground as well as his horse."

"But he's too free with his whip," Alec said critically.

"Perhaps, but he's a great hand rider, too. He's strong and he's able to use his strength in assisting a horse. I've seen him do it a hundred different ways. Horses respond to his urging."

"He's quick to take advantage of any situation," Alec conceded, "that's for sure."

"Because he's smart as well as a strong rider," Henry said. "He knows when to hold the rail behind a horse and when to swing outside, trying to loop him."

"Then you don't think he's going to have any trouble winning this one?" Alec asked.

"I didn't say that," Henry answered, his gaze still following the horses to the post. "Manny is the best rider in the race, but the filly is too green."

The filly was slipping and sliding, giving Manizales a hard time. "But she's game," Henry added. "She can't walk in this stuff, but maybe she'll prove she can run in it. I don't think they'd have her out there otherwise."

"Even so," Alec said, "she only sprinted last year. A mile will probably be too much for her."

"We'll soon find out," Henry said. The chestnut filly along with the others was walking toward the starting gate.

Alec huddled deep within the protection of his warm raincoat. The rain was continuing without letup. Worse still, lightning streaked across the sky and the wind picked up, driving the black clouds overhead. The filly reared in front of the starting gate.

"She's liable to jump out from under Manny," Alec told Henry.

"So might the others," the old trainer commented. It was almost pitch-dark now and the driving rain was whipping across the infield with galelike force.

Alec burrowed deeper into his raincoat. "Maybe the starter will hold them off a moment."

"I doubt it," Henry said. "He's ready to open the gate."

"I'm glad I'm not out there. That wind could sweep you right out of the saddle."

"With no help from your horse," Henry agreed. "I'm glad you're not out there, too. I got a feeling we're going to see some fantastic racing . . . a real *Perils of Pauline* kind of thing."

"What's that?" Alec asked without taking his eyes off the starting gate.

"A movie serial I used to see as a kid. It was a real cliff-hanger, with one stirring climax after another."

"Wow!" A bolt of lightning split the sky, and Alec

was able to distinguish the silks of the riders as their mounts reared in the starting stalls. "I still think the starter ought to hold them off," Alec said.

Henry agreed, saying, "Maybe he'll have to now." Several horses had already backed out of their stalls and were fighting their riders. Henry tried to ignore the storm by concentrating on the horses.

"It's a big field for such a track," he said. "First Command has every right to be the favorite. He likes the distance and can run his race on any sort of footing. But he's too straight in front for my taste. Moonshot is too long-striding for this muddy going, I think. He'll be afraid to stride out. Hayloft won't like the track for the same reason. But Novice moves up in slop like this. Look at him. He looks like a tall bird wading in the water. Nice hind legs, too. . . ."

Henry went on with his comments but Alec kept his eyes on Manizales's chestnut filly, Bitter Sweet. She had a habit of getting into trouble, regardless of the footing, but he wanted her to win.

Another lightning bolt cracked the heavens, and Henry put his hand on Alec's arm. "I want you to watch the way Manizales can whip smoothly with either hand, and the way he switches," he said nervously.

"I don't even carry a whip," Alec said, annoyed at Henry's constant prodding.

"You might someday. Every top rider should know how to switch smoothly. Watch Manizales."

They cringed at the crackle of still another bolt of lightning. Nor were they alone in this. Most of the other huddled spectators were now looking fearfully up at the heavens rather than at the horses.

Alec turned his gaze back to the starting gate. With eight horses in a race there was always danger of a traffic jam under the best of conditions. Today it would be almost miraculous if some fantastic mishaps didn't take place. It would be a difficult race to follow, too. Even under ideal circumstances, watching a race from the stands taxed the eyes of the most experienced among the professional spectators. Few could ever describe exactly what happened during the running of a race, for the pace was too swift. The starting bell would ring, the gate doors would fly open and the stampede would be on. Many dramatic details that won or lost a race—a thrown shoe, a misstep, a bump, a slipped saddle, careless riding—could easily go unnoticed.

Today it would be more difficult than ever to watch everything.

Alec suddenly stiffened, for the horses were now in the gate. There was a great peal of thunder from above, silencing the sound of the starting bell as the gate doors flew open.

...and Hoofs

5

Alec watched the chestnut filly. She had only one horse on her right, being in the next-to-outside post position. While she had always been sluggish getting away, she seemed to want to overdo it this time. She left her stall almost at a walk despite the beating she was taking from Manizales's feet and whip. Then suddenly she wheeled and bolted for the outside rail before Manizales could get her aimed down the stretch.

Suddenly there was a loud shout from the crowd as a horse on the inner rail, also lagging at the break, went down in the slop. The jockey somersaulted over his mount's head and slid like a writhing eel beneath the rail and into the infield.

The horse tried to get up almost instantly, but he had his right foreleg through the knotted reins. He began struggling, but an alert gate crewman dashed over to him and slashed the reins free with a sharp pocketknife. The next moment the horse was being led quickly away while his rider, covered with mud, stomped the infield turf.

Meanwhile, Alec noticed that Manizales had the chestnut filly running strongly after the pack. His feet

were not in his irons, a clear sign that the filly must
almost have thrown him.

"He's riding without stirrups," Alec said.

"I see it. I told you this race would be something,"
Henry answered without removing the binoculars
from his eyes.

Through the beating rain and semi-darkness, the
horses pounded into the first turn. The favorite, First
Command, looked quite at home in the slop, as Henry
had figured, and was in the lead. Behind him were the
others, packed much too closely together and too
mud-spattered to be identifiable. The field swung
wide, some of the horses having trouble getting hold
of the track and slipping dangerously going around the
turn. One jockey, finding no place on the outside to
go, rushed for a narrow opening on the rail. He was
squeezed still more by a tiring horse, who bore in
sharply, slamming against him and causing him to hit
the fence.

Alec saw what was coming even before he heard
Henry's gasp of alarm. The squeezed jockey found out
suddenly that he had no place to go at all. His leg was
being pressed hard against the rail and his horse was
burning his hide on it. The horse lost his running
action and bobbled like an undecided jumper approaching a barrier too high for him; then, as if making
up his mind, he swerved in, jumped the rail and took
his rider into the infield lake.

Henry put down his glasses and said, "Now I've
seen everything. You take them."

Lifting the binoculars to his eyes, Alec ignored the
horse in the lake and focused on the race. Moonshot

passed First Command coming off the first turn and took the lead. But neither horse could get far ahead of the hard-running bunch directly behind. Moving up the backstretch, the two leaders were joined by two more horses who were now running abreast of them.

The chestnut filly was no longer dead-last but picking up horses and moving into fifth place. She might not be able to *walk* in the mud but she was proving she could run! Manizales was keeping her on the rail and saving ground. He started moving her faster as they approached the far turn. Soon, Alec knew, she would be in an all-out drive for the lead.

"Keep your eye on her, Henry!" he said, without offering his friend the binoculars.

"She'll quit," Henry said. "She's too unseasoned." But the excited tone of his voice belied his pessimism.

First Command moved to the front again, trying to steal the race as he went into the far turn. But suddenly he began bearing out, taking the three other leaders part way with him. It was then that Manizales made his move along the rail; there wasn't a thing in the filly's path now that the leaders were veering outside!

She slipped and skidded under Manizales's urging, but made for the gap in the jam ahead. Manizales rocked and pushed her, bending into the turn. He was whipping with his right hand, keeping the filly close to the rail. She was under full steam when First Command caught up and began racing alongside her, his rider, too, scuffing and scrubbing with hands and feet.

The chestnut filly began to inch ahead, getting out of the jam and surging ahead! Alec let out a yell.

"She's not home yet," Henry cautioned.

First Command moved up again, regaining the inches lost to the filly. As soon as she saw him alongside she dug in still more. Manizales was now whipping with his left hand and the other jockey with his right, so that the two horses were hide-scraping as they came off the turn and began their furious contest down the stretch.

Alec watched the filly lose the lead to First Command, then regain it again after a few strides. All in all, the lead changed five times before the two horses reached the final quarter pole.

"Manny hasn't put his whip away since the race started," Alec said.

"He's laying on the leather, all right," Henry agreed. "I counted six belts just coming around the turn."

Through the glasses Alec watched every move of the two horses as they splashed toward the finish line, their riders' silks as black as the rain clouds piled up overhead. For a second his gaze shifted to the jam-packed field directly behind the leaders.

Moonshot and Novice were tucked in along the rail and not out of the race yet. Their riders were rating them lightly and seemed to be waiting for the two leaders to tire.

Approaching the eighth pole, with the finish wire only two hundred and twenty yards away, the chestnut filly faltered and seemed to stumble in the slop. Manizales picked her up quickly with the loss of only a few inches to First Command. Once again he urged her on and she fought back bitterly to regain the lead.

"She's tiring," Alec said.

"Watch Moonshot," Henry said. "His jock is thinking of taking him out and around the filly."

"At a time like this," Alec said, "you don't think. You just ride."

The filly slipped and Alec saw her slide again in the mud. But Manizales didn't touch her with his whip. First Command surged to the front, followed closely by Moonshot who was coming out and around the filly. There was now only a sixteenth of a mile to go. Alec knew Moonshot had little chance of catching First Command, who was driving harder than ever and drawing away.

At the same time, the game chestnut filly still wasn't out of the race. Moonshot had ranged up boldly alongside her but couldn't draw clear. She refused to give way.

But her legs could not match her game spirit, for suddenly her strides faltered again. Gallantly, but with mounting fright, she sought to take hold in the deep slop. She slipped, ducked out and collided with Moonshot. Then, bouncing back, she lost her balance and with sickening swiftness went down in a sprawling heap.

"*Bitter Sweet is down!*" came the cry from the stands.

Alec felt a tautness in his stomach muscles that he recognized only too well—a sensation of surprise, concern, doubt and yet cold-blooded expectancy.

Horses fall and jockeys are thrown on the racetrack. It's part of the game. It's a chance every rider

*takes, every day, under conditions far better than
these.*

Even as the cry arose from the stands, Alec saw
Novice, who was racing directly behind the filly, plow
into her and go down, too, throwing his rider clear.
He tumbled through the murk, sliding beyond the
two prostrate horses, and came to a slithering stop
near the rail. Quickly, he put his hands around the
back of his neck as if to protect himself from the horses
that might run over him. Near him was Manizales—a
crumpled form on the track, his face deep in the mud.

The plunging field behind veered sharply to avoid
the two horses and their riders, some barely clearing
the prone bodies. It was a chilling thing to see, and
the attention of the now silent crowd remained on the
two stricken horses and men rather than on the finish
of the race.

In a minute or two the sprawled figures began to
move. Moonshot climbed to his feet unsteadily; his
rider raised himself to an elbow, then quickly slith-
ered under the rail and got to his feet.

"Those two are all right," Henry said.

The crowd waited for some movement of Manizales's scarlet headpiece to give an indication that the
jockey was conscious. Track officials had reached him
now and were bending over the pitifully small figure.
The filly was trying to get to her feet and some of the
gate crewmen were at her head.

"I think Manny is conscious," Alec said, looking
through the binoculars. "He's just being very careful."

"If it's his neck or back, he should be," Henry said.

"He's had enough falls to know."

The ambulance was now on its way down the track, and Alec said, "Manny has turned his head. He's talking to them."

The filly was up and moving. She wasn't putting much weight on her right foreleg, but that she was using it at all was a good sign. "It's no compound fracture anyway," Henry said. "Maybe they can save her."

The ambulance came to a stop. Moonshot's jockey walked into it, but Manizales was lifted inside on a stretcher. Only when the track was clear again did the crowd relax. They looked at the infield board. First Command had been the winner of the race.

Alec said, "Let's go home. I've had enough for today." He felt sick to his stomach.

Henry studied the boy's face. "We ought to watch a few more, Alec." He didn't like the frightened look he thought he saw in Alec's eyes; one of the best ways to get rid of it was to stick around for a while and watch some races in which there weren't any accidents.

"At least no horses had to be destroyed on the track," Henry added quietly. "That's something. I wouldn't worry much about Manny, either. He's had more than a dozen spills since he's been here, and he always comes up for more."

"I know," Alec said. "I'm sure he'll be okay."

Henry decided to change the subject and talk about the race itself. "Manny might have brought her on," he said. "I think she just might have had enough gameness to come on again and win it."

Alec shrugged his shoulders. "Possibly," he said.

"Well," the old trainer said, picking up his program to consider the horses in the second race, "at least it proved once more that to win a race it's not always enough just to have the best horse."

Alec nodded and, oddly enough, found himself thinking of Steve Duncan. What Henry had just said reminded him that he himself had used almost those very words when Steve had said the best horse made the best rider. Too bad Steve hadn't been here to see this race for himself. It might have convinced him to stay home with his horse Flame, and not go out fanning windmills like a young, reckless Don Quixote.

Bitter Sweet

6

The rain stopped during the night, but the following morning the wind was blowing stiffly out of the north and the temperature was down in the forties. Henry arrived late again, wearing his borrowed topcoat and still complaining of the "unseasonable" weather.

"At least," Alec said, "the track will dry out fast with this wind."

"Nothing could be as bad as yesterday," Henry grunted. "Never have I seen weather like it."

Alec nodded. For him there was more than weather to remember from the day before. A filly with great speed and promise might never race again, and Manizales was in the hospital with a fractured jaw, broken teeth, a concussion and a neck injury. Fortunately, none of the others who had gone down during the running of the first race had been seriously injured.

Henry searched Alec's eyes for any sign of fear. "Did you hear anything new about Manny?" he asked finally.

"Only that they're having a hard time convincing him that he has to stay in the hospital," Alec answered. "With all his injuries he still wants to get back to work."

"Like I said, he's hungry. He'll be back riding before you know it." The trainer paused. "And the filly?"

"She's out for the rest of the year, anyway. Doc's operating on her this morning. She has a slight fracture of the right foreleg. Maybe she'll be able to race again."

"Maybe," Henry repeated doubtfully. "She comes equipped with fragile legs. Gets it from her sire, Polynesian, just as she does her speed. If it didn't happen now, it would've later."

Alec said, "Perhaps so. But you don't get a series of spills like yesterday's very often. She might have splashed home in front if she hadn't collided with Moonshot."

"She ran a game race, all right," Henry agreed. "She was blocked and forced to check sharply several times, but she still came on and tried to bore a hole through the leaders. Yeah, she might have won at that.

"Manny made a lot of trouble for himself and her," Henry went on. "I don't think he needed to ride such a rudderless course. He could have kept her back going into the far turn, then he would have had more left for the stretch run."

"That's hard to say," Alec argued in the other rider's behalf. "Sometimes you get a horse into trouble because you don't know where a traffic tie-up is going to happen. Then when you get in tight quarters and come close to running up on the heels of a horse in front it means you have to check fast. A lot of times your horse won't run again after being stopped."

"You don't get into that kind of a jam if you have enough experience and sense," Henry said. "You know a jam is coming and you stay clear of it . . . or if you stay inside you know you got enough horse under you to take you through a hole before it closes. Manny didn't have that kind of horse under him, so he should've stayed back and waited for the stretch to put her in a drive. That's why I say he asked for what he got."

"What *she* got, too?" Alec asked, his eyes troubled.

"She was in Manny's hands," Henry muttered. "She was just beginning to learn what it was all about. She had enough speed to get a good position and stay out of trouble. That was enough to have going for Manny, more than most riders can figure on. He let her down."

"And he almost got killed doing it," Alec said. "If he hadn't been wearing a skull cap, he'd never be riding again."

"I'm sure of that, too," Henry said quietly. He paused, studied Alec, then added, "That don't need to scare you none."

"I'm always scared," Alec said. "You know me, I never feel confident."

Alec was smiling, so Henry didn't know whether or not to take him seriously. "You shouldn't talk like that, Alec. You settle a horse nice, even a sensitive one like the Black. Everyone knows it."

"That's become a kind of fable now," Alec answered. "You've said it so often people are starting to believe you. I make plenty of mistakes and you know it."

"Maybe so," Henry answered. "But you mostly always rise to the occasion and that's what wins races."

"Horses win races," Alec said quietly. "You trainers make the horses. If we win, you should get the credit. The riders are made by the horses."

Henry studied Alec's face, puzzled by the youth's attitude. "It's funny to hear you talkin' that way, Alec. You've seen plenty of horses that wouldn't put out unless they were forced to turn on speed by their riders. There are plenty of cases where a horse and his trainer would be nothing without the right boy on his back."

"I've heard you say otherwise," Alec reminded his old friend. "You've said often that there really wasn't much difference in top riders."

"No, I only said there was less difference now than when I was riding," Henry said. "A jock could get away with a lot more at the old barrier than in today's starting gate. We had no film patrol in those days, either. Sometimes, in fact most times, it got pretty rough out there. Take a look at some of the old pictures and you'll find most jocks riding with sharp spurs and carryin' big whips which we used plenty any way we could to win a race. Yeah, horses and riders really went through a drilling in those days."

"We're not exactly being coddled today," Alec said quietly, and that ended the subject.

Later in the morning, Alec opened the tack-room trunk and removed a white envelope. Inside were several small wads of cotton, adhered to which were tiny granular bits of dirt and dried blood. This was what Doc Palmer had cut out of the Black's injured hoof several months ago. It had been the source of all the horse's trouble; once it was out and the cut healed everything had been fine.

Alec put the wads back in the envelope. He couldn't have said exactly why he was saving them, except, perhaps, as a reminder to himself and particularly to Henry that everything was in good shape and they could race the Black. As he left the room he ran into Henry. "Come on," he said. "We ought to watch the operation on Bitter Sweet."

"Why?" the trainer asked uneasily.

"It's something we should know about," Alec said. "Part of our job, like you're always telling me."

"I don't like to watch operations, even on a horse."

"I didn't know you were sensitive about them," Alec said. He tried not to smile. "What about the tough old days you were telling me about, when a horse with a fractured leg was destroyed right on the track? Was that easier to watch?"

"That was different. Some people just don't like to watch operations. I happen to be one of 'em."

"It's not as bad as you make it sound. I think you ought to come along with me. You're never too old to learn something new. That's what you've always said."

Henry fidgeted, and there was a strained, uneasy silence between them. Finally, the old man said, "Okay, I'll go if that's the way you want it."

They left Hialeah Park through the Barn Gate, waited for the traffic light to change, then hurriedly crossed the street. Walking beside Alec, Henry straightened his blocklike figure and made a gallant attempt to look unconcerned about the whole thing. He would have preferred turning down Alec's invitation to witness the operation on Bitter Sweet. It was one thing to know that veterinary surgery had progressed to the point where a horse's broken bones could be mended, and quite another thing to watch it being done. Still, as Alec had said, whatever he witnessed should be easier to take than watching a horse destroyed on the track.

"Racehorses were lots tougher in the old days," he said suddenly in an attempt to regain his position of authority. "Their legs held up even though they raced much more often. I've seen 'em race twice in one day with only a half-hour rest in between. They don't come like that any more. They're too coddled."

Alec smiled, thinking of the tender way in which Henry had been treating the Black during the past few months. He believed, too, that today's racehorses were much improved over the old-time runners Henry was always talking about. They were better trained, faster and more efficient, just as the sport itself was better. There were automatic starting gates to get the horses away in a line and without delay, film patrols to prevent rough, unscrupulous riding tactics, and safety helmets, to say nothing of modern veterinary surgery, which they were about to witness.

They came to a stop before a one-story concrete-block building which was the veterinary hospital. Henry led the way inside but, Alec noted, his face couldn't have been paler if he'd been going to his own operation.

The outer office was heated and a young woman was the only occupant. She glanced up from her typewriter, smiled at Alec and said, "You're a little late. They've already put her up on the operating table. You'd better hurry."

"Thanks, Miss Clay. I tried to get here sooner, but . . ." He paused, glancing at Henry. "This is Henry Dailey," he added. "Henry, Miss Clay, Dr. Palmer's secretary."

"I know," she said. "The trainer of the Black couldn't possibly be a stranger to anyone. You've got yourself a wonderful horse, Mr. Dailey." Her pale blue eyes studied the old man.

"He's made up for a lot of disappointments during my life," Henry returned quietly. He didn't like the way she seemed to be sizing him up. She was too composed while he was squirming inwardly. He was certain she knew how he felt about being there.

She smiled, trying to make it easier for him. "Racing is a great game. I meet so many interesting people, each so different in his own way."

"I'm sure you do," Henry said, following Alec toward another door. He tried to return her smile and to appear as casual as she seemed to be about this business of operating on horses. "Having a great horse like the Black makes me really appreciate racing," he added. "And believe me, Miss, I'm going to do all I can to keep him out of this place."

"I hope so," Miss Clay said quickly. "I do hope you will, Mr. Dailey."

The next room was a laboratory, at the moment unoccupied, filled with cases of shining instruments.

Alec strode through toward a door leading to a room beyond but Henry held back, his eyes on the instrument cases.

"Come on," Alec said impatiently. "Miss Clay said we're late already."

"It must be like operating on a human being," the old man said uneasily, his face ashen-white. "Maybe we ought not, Alec . . . I mean, I never did like surgery."

Henry tried to meet Alec's gaze and failed miserably. How could he explain to him that he was plain scared? To him surgery meant these gleaming, sharp instruments and an amphitheater tense with the drama of life and death. It meant a hushed, ominous silence and rubber gloves on a surgeon's skilled hands. It meant a shining scalpel and spurting blood. He was scared because it was all too easy, at his age, to see himself on an operating table.

Alec said quietly, "There's nothing to be frightened about. You've been watching too many TV medic shows."

"It's not that," the old man said. He shifted his weight from one foot to the other, ill at ease. "It's just that I don't like the atmosphere," he added a little defiantly.

"I don't either, not especially," Alec said.

"I'm not so sure about that. You've been over here before." Henry tried to grin and almost succeeded. "You know," he continued, bidding for more time, "you're something like another rider I once knew. He'd been in and out of hospitals so often with race injuries that he got to liking the atmosphere and he began going there on his days off. He enjoyed watching the surgeons at work. Finally, they let him put on a white gown and he did everything but operate."

"Maybe he missed his calling," Alec said. "Maybe he'd rather have been a surgeon than a rider. But that's not why I'm here," he added, slightly irritated by Henry's squeamishness. "I'm going inside. You do what you like."

When Alec had gone, Henry quietly faced the closed door separating them. For several minutes he didn't move, fighting the panic within him. Then, furious with himself for what he knew *had* to be needless fear, he wrenched the door open and strode inside the operating room.

He saw the filly, Bitter Sweet, lying on the operating table, arc lights blazing above her and white-gowned men standing around the table. A small group of spectators hovered nearby. His nerves tingling, Henry nodded to some of the horsemen he knew. They paid little attention to him, all being interested in the work of the veterinary surgeon, and for this he was grateful.

For a while Henry kept his eyes on Dr. Palmer's tall, round-shouldered figure, hoping thus to reassure himself, even though the man was well known to be competent and skillful. But finally his gaze shifted to the curving line of faces just beyond the operating table. He picked out Alec's and moved over to stand beside him.

Alec hoped that within a few minutes Henry would see this operation for what it really was—no curtain raiser, no impending TV drama but a quick, efficient, skillful job of mending a horse's broken bone. The large doors at the far end of the room were slightly open and some neighborhood kids were peeking inside. Perhaps one of them would be a veterinary surgeon himself one day, Alec thought.

He knew that the filly had come through those doors a short time ago, quietly and without pain. She had been given a sedative, nothing more than a tranquilizer that a human being would have taken under the same circumstances. Once she was inside the room, the anesthesia had been injected intravenously, and as it began to take effect she had been carefully lowered to the operating table, which lay flush with the floor. She had been secured, then the hydraulic lift had elevated the table so that the surgeon could go to work.

She was resting comfortably now, and the anesthesia was being maintained by a closed-circuit, circle-type machine. She breathed easily through the mask about her nose, the tubes of the mask leading through a vaporizer and into a large rubber bag that contained a mixture of gas and oxygen. It moved like a living thing as she inhaled and exhaled.

An operating sheet, draped over the filly's injured leg, had a rectangular, open window which exposed the area ready for incision. Her leg had been shaved and painted with an antiseptic.

Dr. Palmer finished drying his hands on a sterile towel; he glanced at his assistant standing alongside and nodded. They were masked and gowned and scrubbed, ready to begin. The surgeon's eyes swept over the table and he made a swift, meticulous inventory of his instruments.

Henry muttered, "It's like watching them operate on a member of your family."

Alec didn't answer. He was aware of a faint smell of ozone coming from the ultraviolet lamps, which he knew could effectively kill bacteria in the air. But he also knew that the greatest advance in preventing infection during veterinary surgery had come with the discovery of sulpha drugs and penicillin and strepto-mycin.

While the assistant injected novocaine into the injured area, the surgeon glanced around and nodded to Alec and Henry. Then he took the razor-edged scalpel and bent over the table.

Henry turned away from the scene but Alec continued watching. There was a powerful light directly above the operating table which cast no shadow, generated no heat. The surgeon had a square piece of gauze in one hand and he pressed it hard against the exposed area before making his incision. The scalpel slashed quickly to bone level. His assistant steadied the filly's leg and removed the rush of blood with a suction tube which he rotated in the depths of the wound. When the opening showed clear, the surgeon swabbed it dry and packed it with cotton. The injured bone area was now in complete view.

"I have all the room I need," the surgeon told his assistant. Then his gloved fingers probed the wound for bone fragments and adhesions at the fracture site. He paused to allow his assistant to manipulate the suction tube again, then walked over to look at the x-ray plate that was hanging against the wall. It showed a fracture of the long bone.

It wasn't good, but he'd seen a lot worse during the past week. The filly had a fifty-fifty chance of ever racing again. Postoperative care of these weight-carrying bones was always the big problem. But that would come later. Right now he had to join the fractured parts perfectly and make certain the leg would stay that way long enough for a firm callous formation to develop. Fortunately, the filly was young and the healing process would not take as long as with an aged horse. That was one thing in her favor, anyway.

He went back to the table. "How's she doing, Max?" he asked, turning to the anesthetist.

The report came quickly. "Pulse and respiration have steadied, Bill. Go ahead."

The anesthetist was a big man who kept shifting his weight from one foot to the other while adjusting the small machine before him. When the adjusting was finished, he glanced at the heart monitor attached to the machine. Satisfied, he straightened and waited for the surgeon to proceed.

Alec, who had been watching the anesthetist, left the small group and went over to him. "What gas are you using?" he asked.

"Halothane," Max answered, his eyes studying Alec from beneath heavy brows. "Ever hear of it?"

"I've read about it," Alec answered. "It has twice the strength of chloroform and four times that of ether, so less of it has to be used."

A smile crossed the man's face. "You're right," he

said quietly, his eyes leaving Alec for the heart monitor. "More expensive but worth it, and a big step forward. No danger of any explosive mixtures as with ether. No effect on the heart, liver or kidneys as with chloroform. It allows the muscles to maintain complete relaxation, too. Just look at her," he added, satisfied and proud of his work.

The filly lay absolutely still as the operation proceeded. The anesthetist was an important part of this skillful team, Alec knew. He would keep the filly under anesthesia as long as necessary, using the halothane sparingly but effectively. He would add oxygen to supply her body's needs and watch for any sudden change in heartbeat, blood pressure and pulse.

She was breathing easily, Alec noted, the large rubber bag rising and falling regularly. The mask over her upper and lower jaw was airtight. She inhaled through one tube and exhaled through the other. The controls were set, regulating the amount of halothane and oxygen which she was breathing in. All carbon dioxide was being removed by soda lime contained in a metal cannister. Everything was going on schedule. The moments passed quickly and there was no sound within the room but the clink of operating instruments.

Finally, the surgeon selected vitallium screws of the size needed to secure the fractured bone firmly. He inserted them into the bone with a small drill, and the whirring noise from the machine suddenly dominated the room.

Alec glanced at Henry and found that he had turned

away momentarily from the table. The whirring of the drill stopped as the surgeon had an x-ray technician take a quick picture. A few minutes later, the surgeon was looking at a film, still wet, that showed the progress of his work. Satisfied, he picked up his drill again. The screws he was inserting would remain in the bone permanently.

Suddenly the anesthetist said, "Hold it a minute, Bill." He began adjusting a valve.

The surgeon waited, brushing the sweat from his forehead. "How's she doing?" he asked after a few minutes.

"Pulse was slowing up but it's steady again."

"Shall I go ahead?"

"You'd better wait a couple more minutes," the big man answered. He adjusted the line to increase the flow of oxygen, then watched the rubber bag. The filly was breathing regularly but he wanted to make certain no complications developed. He had lost one horse this season at Hialeah but he attributed that death to surgical shock rather than respiratory failure. However, he wasn't taking any chances with this one. She was a good filly with years ahead of her as a fine broodmare, even if she didn't make the races again.

Alec turned his gaze to the elderly, gnomelike man standing closest to the table of any of the spectators. He was the filly's groom and, Alec knew, was taking this harder than anyone else. He had twisted his cap in his hands; his bared head was completely bald except for a fringe of shaggy white hair. He was breathing in vast gulps of air as if this would help his filly in her own breathing. Now he rubbed his big nose

with the cap—an attempt, Alec knew, to hide the
concern and fear he felt.

Most caretakers were like this man, Alec reflected.
They went from track to track, from youth to old age,
caring only for their beloved charges and the day's
eating money. On the whole they were a happy lot.
But they were quick to adjust to whatever tomorrow
would bring, for that was their way, too.

The surgeon looked over at the groom and said,
"Dick, you have nothing to worry about. She'll be
back in a year."

"I sure hope so, Doc. They'll send her to the farm,
don't you think?"

"It'll be the best place for her. She won't be able to
move out of her stall for three months, anyway."

"Just fix her up so she'll be back sometime, Doc."
The powerful overhead light disclosed the purple
veins in the little man's nose. He rubbed it again.
"That's all I want. I'll be waitin' for her. You jus' fix her
up."

"We'll fix her up all right," the surgeon said. Then,
with glances, he invited the others to listen to what he
had to say next while waiting for word from the
anesthetist to proceed. "What helps us in this case is
that because she fell she couldn't continue the race.
We have real trouble when a horse fractures a leg and
keeps running on it. Horses' bones are brittle compared to ours and when one is fractured in a race it can
break into splintered fragments, especially when the
horse tries to keep running."

The anesthetist interrupted. "You can go ahead

now, Bill," he said. "Pulse and respiration are back to normal."

The surgeon continued with his work. When he had finished drilling, the two screws were securely and correctly imbedded in the bone. He had done everything he could. All that was left now was to close the wound and put on a plaster of Paris cast to give the screws added support and to immobilize the injured leg as much as possible. Unfortunately, it was almost impossible for a horse to keep its weight off a fractured leg for any length of time, and this made successful treatment more difficult than in the case of a human being.

The surgeon's assistant handed Dr. Palmer the needle with suture attached and, stitching neatly, he closed the wound. Then he gave the filly another antibiotic injection to combat infection and, removing the operating sheet, applied sulfanilimide powder thickly to the hair around the wound, rubbing it into the skin also to prevent superficial bacterial infections. Next, his assistant helped him put an orthopedic stockinet over the leg. He made certain it was absolutely smooth before applying the wet plaster of Paris bandage. He wound it quickly but efficiently about the leg until he was satisfied the cast would provide maximum support and an even pressure.

At last he straightened up. "Okay, John. We're done," he said to his assistant. Then he called to his anesthetist, "Turn her off, Max."

Alec stepped back as the big man turned off his machine and removed the mask from the filly's mouth.

All the other operating equipment had been removed from the table, and now the hydraulic lift lowered the filly to the floor, where she was left to lie quietly and unrestrained in a relaxed, tranquilized state.

The small group began breaking up, speaking to one another in quiet, almost hushed voices as if there were a continued need for silence. Only when the surgeon laughed loudly at something someone said to him did they suddenly start raising their voices. But they kept away from the filly, giving her the room and air she needed.

"How long before she'll be up?" Alec asked the anesthetist, having noticed a quick twitching of the filly's legs.

"They usually come out of this gas pretty fast," the man said, putting his equipment away. "Most of them are up within a half-hour. A few take longer."

Henry came across the room to stand beside Alec; he said nothing, his eyes on the filly.

"Do they come out of it quietly or struggling?" Alec asked.

"Quietly," the big man answered. "I've only seen a few excited ones. That's another advantage of halothane."

Alec turned to Henry, whose face had a sickly pallor. "Shall we wait or do you want to go now?" he asked.

"I think we ought to go," Henry answered.

They were nearing the door when Dr. Palmer stopped them. "Nice to have had you here, Henry," he said.

"A good filly, game as they come," Henry answered. "Too bad about her."

"Don't cross her off so fast," the veterinarian said. "She could be back in training before the year's out."

"I hope so, Doc," Henry said sincerely. "I sure do." He took another few steps toward the door.

"You come back, hear?" the veterinarian called to him.

"Yeah, Doc, sure." Henry left the operating room sure of only one thing. He wasn't *ever* going back unless he had to. And the only way to make certain of staying out of that room was to keep the Black as sound as a dollar. But how sound was that any more? One couldn't be sure of anything these days. He rubbed the horse chestnuts that he carried in his pocket for good luck.

First Start

7

Henry showed up at the track earlier than usual the following morning. "I'm having the horseshoe man come around," he told Alec.

That was enough to let Alec know that during the night Henry had arrived at a decision concerning the Black's program. New shoes had been put on only two weeks ago and Henry rarely changed plates so soon unless the Black was going to race.

"What made you change your mind?" he asked. He didn't want to appear too anxious, just interested—perhaps even a little puzzled—in the hope of drawing Henry out.

"That one thirty-seven mile on the grass the other morning," Henry said quietly.

"I thought you said it was too fast."

"It was. But it was a big move to me; he handled that soft turf perfectly. It convinced me he was ready."

"I see," Alec said, although actually he didn't. He'd never be able to understand how Henry could be furious about something Alec had done one day and forget about it completely the next. "When are we going then?" he asked.

"There's a mile race on the grass tomorrow, so let's

blow him out this morning for it."

"Great!" Alec said, no longer trying to conceal his joy. "How far do I take him?" He could smell the pine tar in the body brace a groom was using a few stalls away.

"Three-eighths. Take him over the main track, breaking from the gate. He's been away from it for some time, and it won't do no harm to have him see it again. Have him look things over now instead of when he has to get out of there fast. Take your time, just walk him in and out, if you think he's curious. Break him when he's good and ready."

"Okay," Alec said.

"Pull him up after an eighth from the gate. Hobby-horse him until the quarter pole, then let him go again. That'll blow him out good."

"Fine," Alec said. "You want to saddle up now or wait for the new plates?"

"We'll go now. The horseshoer won't be around until later. We'll save the new plates for the race. It'll give him better leverage and traction when he needs it most. No sense wearing down the toe grab and calk now."

The sun had climbed a little higher, turning to gold in the eastern sky. Henry gave Alec a leg up and swung him into the saddle. "He likes the warmer weather," the old man said.

"Yeah," Alec said, knotting the reins as the Black shifted quickly beneath him. "He's full of go this morning."

"He should be. He's done nothing but walk the last couple of days."

"I might have trouble snugging him up," Alec said, "like last time."

"You don't need to snug him up too slow. I want him blown out good."

Alec left Henry at the gap in the fence and rode slowly toward the starting gate at the far end of the backstretch. The Black's hoofs made a flat, wet, rhythmic sound on the pock-marked track. He handled easily, making no attempt to break away, but Alec shortened his reins still more and rose higher in his irons.

"Easy, mister," he said softly. He didn't want the Black getting away from him this morning. It was just as well that the coming race would be over grass. It suited Alec as well as the Black, being a welcome change from dirt racing. It used to be that infield courses were mostly confined to steeplechasing with only an occasional flat race over the grass. But during the last ten years most tracks had inaugurated turf classics with large purses. The Hialeah Turf Cup, for example, was worth close to one hundred thousand dollars. Also, the large number of foreign horses being imported and raced in the United States were, in a way, responsible for the ever-mounting popularity of races over the infield course. Abroad, they didn't race on dirt tracks at all.

Alec was nearly at the starting gate. He slowed down the Black still more in order to stay clear of the horses coming down the track. When they swept by, the Black kicked his heels in the air.

"Okay," Alec said, "your turn's coming now."

The track in front of the starting gate was a sea of

slop. The crew had been schooling young horses all morning and, Alec figured, were pretty tired of all the activity in such deep going. The men were squishing through the mud, and one yelled, "Hiya, Alec. It's been a long time." The man's black rubber rain pants were splattered with mud. He came forward to take the Black's bridle.

"Better let me take him in alone, John," Alec said. "I just want him to look around a minute. We'll walk in and out once."

"Okay, Alec. I'll stand by."

Alec patted the Black. He had him under control and didn't expect any trouble. But one never could be sure. Going back of the gate, he moved him carefully toward the starting stall.

"Now, take it easy," he said soothingly. The track crew were standing far enough away and carrying on a conversation among themselves.

"You goin' fishin' later this morning, John?" Alec heard one ask.

"If it clears up I will, and if I get away from here in time."

"Maybe this is the last of the breakers."

"Maybe it is. It's been a long morning so far."

"He'll leave here in a hurry, and there's no more business coming up." The long chute was empty of other horses.

Alec rode the Black into the stall and John closed the door behind them. The Black looked through the grilled gate but made no attempt to break through it.

Alec continued patting and gentle-talking him. "That's it," he said quietly. "Just look around all you want; that's all you have to do." The stall quarters were confining but the Black didn't seem to object. He was neither nervous nor curious. He was only eager to be turned free.

Alec saw John climbing the gate's framework. "He's okay," he called. "Open up and let us out again."

The rear door was opened and, reluctantly but steadily, the Black backed out. Alec patted him again and took him around in a large circle. "Okay, John," he called. "We're going this time."

Once more the Black moved inside the gate and the door was closed behind him. He pitched his ears forward when Alec, crouching low in the saddle, placed more weight on his withers. The gate would open any second.

Alec took a shorter hold of the reins. He didn't want the Black to come out too fast. There must be no sudden strain that might injure his horse and keep him from the race on the following day.

"Easy, mister," he kept repeating. He wanted him to come out slowly and find his stride; then he'd let him run for an eighth of a mile before pulling him up. He'd try to keep him at a slow gallop, as Henry wanted, until they reached the quarter pole. Then he'd let him go against the bit again.

The metal doors clanged open, and the starter's bell rang. The Black leaped forward. Alec sat very still, waiting for his horse to settle in stride. He inched up the reins, yet the Black's strides lengthened, eating up track before him; he shook his head, seeking relief from the snug hold on his mouth.

Alec allowed the leather to slip a little through his

hands. He wanted to restrain the Black without making him furious, just as he wanted a fast eighth of a mile but not a blistering one. After their last workout, he had to be extra careful not to let the Black get away from him.

They flashed by the eighth pole and the sprint was over. Alec drew back on the reins, asking for obedience rather than demanding it; his snug hold became a tight one. He talked to the Black, his head close to the stallion's.

The Black slowed down, his ears flicking to the front and then to the back as he listened to Alec. He never stopped asking for more rein but he did slacken his speed as he rounded the far turn and moved into the homestretch.

The Black snorted at sight of the long, empty stands and dug his hoofs deep into the mud, sending it splaying behind him. When he passed the quarter pole, there was a sudden release of the metal against his mouth. He went up against the bit, his speed coming with electrifying swiftness in his newly found freedom!

Alec leaned forward, his head beside the Black's, and let him go. His horse ran for the sheer love of running and Alec shared his love with him.

The finish pole swept by and the final quarter mile had ended. Alec sat back in the saddle when the stallion slowed down and the tempo of his hoofs was reduced to a flat, squishing sound in the mud.

An hour later Henry had entered the Black in the turf race on the following day's program. He wouldn't know who the other entries were until the list came off the mimeographing machine later in the day. Nor would he know, until then, how much weight the Black would be assigned. Henry considered the race only a "prep" for the longer, more important stake races to come. The Black was fresh, his eighth of a mile from the gate in 11-2/5ths seconds had been done very handily, and his sizzling final quarter in 22 seconds was even more impressive. He would race well tomorrow, and the next time he would be better still. The race would do more to condition him than three or four morning workouts.

The evening newspapers carried the story of the Black's surprise entry in the overnight race, and a sports columnist wrote:

> The mighty Black is slated to make his first appearance of the year in tomorrow's sixth race at a mile distance over the infield turf course. The $5,000 purse is the smallest for which the champion, who has been training in track record time, has ever raced. He was "blown out" an eighth this morning in 11-2/5 and went a final quarter in :22, with his regular rider Alec Ramsay in danger of having his arms pulled from their sockets.
>
> Trainer Henry Dailey's problem right along has been to keep the Black active enough without having him too sharp too early. There is little doubt that the champion will benefit from tomorrow's race although he has been assigned what is believed to be the heaviest burden given a handicap horse for his first start of the year on a major track.
>
> The Black will carry a backbreaking impost of 136

pounds. Despite this burden he is sure to be the
favorite of what track officials believe will be the
largest crowd of the season. Those who have not seen
the Black in his morning trials will find him looking
every bit the champion he is and, in this writer's
opinion, fully capable of giving ten to twenty-five
pounds to the formidable (but outclassed) group he is
expected to oppose in tomorrow's race.

Henry Dailey plans no more prep races for the
Black, whose next start following tomorrow's race will
probably be the $75,000 added Hialeah Turf Cup on
February 19 at a mile and one-half.

Henry didn't read the evening newspapers, only
the mimeographed sheet he'd picked up from the
racing secretary's office. He went over the names of
the entries, their weight assignments and post posi-
tions. He didn't like the 136 pounds assigned to the
Black, but the great stallion had proved often that he
had the ability to carry weight over a distance; he had
lugged as much as 146 pounds and still beaten top
horses. Even so, it was a lot of weight to put on a horse
the first time out.

Henry conceded to Alec that the Black didn't have
much to beat. With a couple of exceptions, tomorrow's
field was distinctly a second-rate bunch. Most of the
horses couldn't carry their speed much over three-
quarters of a mile. What bothered him most of all was
the post position they'd drawn. They were number 1,
the inside post position. It was not a good spot for a
first start, especially against horses with a lot of early
speed who would, most likely, break in front and try

to take the lead. He didn't want the Black jammed inside. For a few moments he considered scratching his horse from the race, then decided against it. He had procrastinated long enough. The Black would go to the post.

At four-fifteen the afternoon of the following day Alec rode the Black into the starting gate. The atmosphere was entirely different from that during the morning hours, but the presence of other horses and crewmen scrambling busily about the gate's framework didn't bother the Black.

He had been the first horse to enter the gate, and he stood quietly in post position number 1 while Alec talked to him and waited. There were eleven horses in the race, a surprisingly large field considering the Black's presence. Alec supposed they were there because every owner and trainer knew that it was possible for *any* horse to beat a champion if the circumstances were right; and this was the Black's first start of the year when anything might happen.

Displaying his first sign of impatience, the tall stallion tossed his head and shifted his feet nervously within the close confines of the starting stall. Alec patted him soothingly. The longer he had to stand in the narrow stall, the more nervous he was likely to become.

Suddenly, the white-faced chestnut in the second stall reared. His rider, Willy Walsh, used all his strength to bring the horse down, but it was of no use. Finally the jockey grabbed the sides of the stall and got clear of the rearing horse while a crewman grabbed hold of his head and, after a brief struggle, succeeded in getting him down. Slowly and carefully the jockey eased himself back into the saddle.

"You okay, Willy?" the starter called from his high perch beside the gate.

"Yeah," the jockey answered. "I'm all right." His high treble voice rose above the shouting of the other riders.

The Black was affected by the mounting excitement and shifted his feet more nervously than ever. Alec continued patting him while watching the chestnut in the next stall; that horse might try to do another back flip which would only make things worse. Willy Walsh was having a rough time, for his mount was running his race in the gate; he wouldn't have much stamina left if he kept it up. The chestnut was a sprinter and should not be a factor in a mile race. On the other hand, Alec knew that *any* horse could go *any* distance if the race was run slowly enough. Again, the outcome of the race depended upon the circumstances under which it was run.

Alec readjusted his goggles and glanced down the line. Most of the other horses were filing into the gate as if they were being led to the feed tub. No trouble at all now. The big bay in the fourth stall had his head down and looked as if he might be falling asleep. His rider was trying to shake him out of it by yanking his head and kicking him in the belly. Alec knew the horse to be one who might well be left at the post but who could go a distance and ran best from behind.

The white-faced chestnut in the second stall reared again and a crewman scrambled over the framework to grab his head. Once more Willy Walsh was lucky to get out of the saddle in time, and Alec caught the other's gaze as he clung to the side of the stall, the twelve-hundred-pound chestnut rearing and plunging alongside.

Luck's all, Alec thought. *How well it applies to most of us here. If Willy had been a little slower sliding off, he'd be under those hoofs instead of where he is. And if the chestnut comes out at the break and slams into us, we might end up in the infield lake. If we'd been lucky and drawn any other position but number 1, we'd have fewer horses to run through and around in this big field. Now we've got to try and get away fast enough to go inside in the dash to the first bend. No wonder most jocks say they'd rather be lucky than good. Anyway, if I have to make mistakes I hope they're the right ones. I don't want to lose this race by leaving the gate too slowly. I've got to get racing room somewhere and I've got to be slippery. I'm riding a champion but I can still get into plenty of trouble. So can Willy Walsh and every rider in this race. You need luck to keep going. It takes more than skill to stay alive.*

Alec waited for the crew to load the last few horses into the gate, meanwhile fighting off any thought of what might possibly happen to him during the running of the race. He knew it was the same with the others, even though they never talked about it. Each rider had his own secret way of fighting off fear. It was perfectly normal and natural, considering what they faced, for any horse could be a rider's last. Such knowledge was part and parcel of their trade. They accepted it with their first assignment on a racehorse. They knew that of all those connected with racing, they were the only ones who were expected to go for their lives as well as for money. Whatever amount they received during the course of a day's racing was not enough . . . not in money, anyway.

Alec decided he'd better think about something else. The weather was right for the races. Some 35,000 persons were assembled in the tiered stands and mezzanines and galleries. The well-manicured hedge was directly to his left, and beyond it could be seen a man in a silver-and-black gondola, sculling his way over the waters of the infield lake. Flamingos waded nearby undisturbed by the gondolier's presence. It was a peaceful, quiet scene in contrast to what was going on in the starting gate and the clamoring grandstand.

All but the heads of the number 10 and 11 horses were lined up now, Alec noted. *Only a few more tense seconds to wait.* He patted the Black. He talked to him. He heard the high-pitched cries of the jockeys and the instructions from the starter. Across his mind flitted an image of the gondolier, wearing a large straw hat with a red band, and a white sailor's shirt with a bright red handkerchief about his neck.

Alec's gaze was on the official starter. Any second now he'd press the button which would open the doors. Just beyond, an assistant starter held a red flag high in the air, ready to drop it at the sound of the starting bell. Alec forgot about the colorful gondolier, the watching multitude, everything but the race itself.

The Black was on his toes and ready. He had to get

out of there fast, Alec decided, for if the others outran him to the first turn he'd surely be in trouble.

"No chance, sir! Not yet," Willy Walsh's high-pitched cry came from the next stall. The white-faced chestnut was turned sideways, and a crewman hurriedly straightened him out.

Suddenly, the grilled doors clanged open. The starting bell rang. The red flag came down. All the riders yelled as one, "Yah! Yah! Yah!"

The Black and the white-faced chestnut broke together, their plunging bodies brushing together slightly in their eagerness to get away. Alec felt the impact, but it didn't bother him for he knew that his own weight was perfectly balanced over the Black's withers where it wouldn't hinder his mount's action. He urged the Black on, determined to get in the clear and set a pace which would convince the other jockeys it was much too fast for them to follow.

The chestnut racing alongside jumped at a shadow on the track and lost a little ground to the Black, but he came on again with Willy Walsh rocking in the saddle and pumping his legs as if determined to stay with the Black. Just behind the two leaders, the large field of horses spread across the track.

Alec decided not to push the Black any more until he had found his stride. They were almost free and clear, almost out of trouble. The chestnut racing a stride behind couldn't hold his speed, and the others had left the post raggedly and slow.

As they approached the first turn, the chestnut jumped at another mark in the track. This time he lost more ground and stumbled as he sought to regain his hold in the soft turf. He staggered sideways, brushing against the Black's flanks.

Alec shortened rein quickly, pulling up the Black and steadying him as the two horses collided.

He glanced at Willy Walsh when the chestnut bounced off to one side and stumbled again. Willy's face was taut with fear. He started to slip from the saddle and then managed to regain his balance. Alec loosened a wrap on the reins, wanting to draw clear of the wobbling chestnut and slip away. He was making his move when he saw Willy lose his balance again. Quickly, he reached over and helped steady the jockey.

It took no more than flashing seconds to help the other rider, but the field was thundering upon them when Alec turned the Black free and bent into the first turn. The Black drew out to a lead of a length over the bunched field. Alec let him maintain this lead until they came flying off the turn and entered the backstretch. There he took up another notch in the reins and rode his horse under a snug hold.

But the Black did not want a breather. He could hear the sound of hoofbeats behind him. He shook his head, demanding more rein. Alec did not let him have it. The pace being set was unusually fast for the mediocre field they were racing today, and even under a snug hold the Black was putting more and more distance between himself and the other horses.

Only when they were approaching the far turn did Alec relent and let loose a notch in the reins. The big stallion plunged forward, shifting into high speed with a smoothness that left Alec in awe, as it always did, no matter how often he rode him. He moved into the turn with giant strides, staying close to the inner hedge as if he knew from past experience that it was the shortest way home. Alec glanced back and it seemed to him that the other horses were traveling backward! He found himself clucking to the Black without there being any need for it. He felt nothing but an overwhelming joy that made every racing risk seem worthwhile. He gave the Black another wrap of rein.

From the stands came a mounting roar. The Black's ears, which had been pinned back against his head, flicked forward at the sound and his strides came faster and longer.

Midway down the homestretch, Alec crossed the reins again and shortened his hold. Henry would have his head if he won this race by more than a sixteenth of a mile! Henry didn't believe in toying with opposition, good or bad though it might be. "Go fast enough to win without getting into any trouble," had been his orders. "I don't want you humiliating other people's horses."

Alec took up on the reins a little more. He'd have a fight on his hands if he shortened them any further. Even with his neck bowed by the tight hold, the stallion continued moving away from the field with ease. When they had left the finish line behind, Alec reined in his horse until he got him to stop. Then, turning him around, he jogged back toward the roaring stands. He had won by too much but had never been happier. It had been a long time since he had felt this way. It was good to be back.

On Camera

8

The film of the feature race at Hialeah was run over Miami television stations that evening, and a popular sportscaster said, "The Black proved today that he is a horse for all seasons and for all courses. He toyed with a formidable, if outclassed, field and gave full notice to the cream of the handicap ranks that he is ready to defend his championship title at any time. The thirty-five thousand people on hand to witness the Black's return to the races were treated to a record-breaking mile on the grass. His time was one thirty-four, a new American record.

"Many noted trainers and track personalities in the crowd had had their doubts that the Black was ready for a top effort. He dispelled that notion quickly and dramatically, taking the lead at the break and accelerating like a runaway express. He continued to draw out throughout the race and had the crowd gasping at his performance. There is no doubt that he is at the top of his form and that there are few horses in America, if any, who can stay with him."

A moment later the screen showed the Black in the winner's circle, wheeling and fractious, with people milling about him. The sportscaster said, "As you can see, the Black saved his clowning until the race was over. He did not like the battery of photographers' flashes popping around him in the overpopulated circle. You might say that the showmanship he's displaying here is almost equal to his race performance."

The film ended and Henry, watching the program in his motel room, started to turn off the TV. Alec stopped him as the sportscaster continued. "In the Bahamas, however, there just might be a horse with which the Black must reckon. At Nassau the winner of the Cup race was the island-bred Flame. His time over a mile on the grass was also one thirty-five. It is doubtful, however, that his time will be recognized since Nassau racing is unsanctioned by parent organizations. There have been many 'phantom' race horses in the past from the islands but none ever credited, however dubiously, with such a mark. It may well be that Flame's win, coming on the day of the Black's victory over the same distance, might mean a match in the offing. At least, it offers an exciting prospect if Hialeah's press agentry extends an invitation to the Bahamian Cup winner.

"Tomorrow night we'll be devoting this program to a round-table discussion with some of the leading jockeys now racing at Hialeah. We hope you'll be with us. This is 'Count' Cornwell. Good night, all."

Henry turned off the set and said, "I still don't think you should appear on that show tomorrow night. Cornwell can make an interview pretty rough."

Alec didn't answer and Henry repeated his remark. Only then did the boy look up, his face thoughtful.

"I'm sorry, Henry," he apologized. "I was thinking of that horse Flame."

"What horse Flame?"

"The one who won at Nassau today. The one Cornwell just talked about."

"Oh, that one. Phantom horses are a dime a dozen in the islands."

"This one's no phantom. He belongs to Steve Duncan."

"Who's Steve Duncan?"

"The fellow who wrote me. The one who came to see me. I told you."

"What's he doin' in Nassau then?"

"Racing."

"That's obvious." Henry studied Alec's face. "You mean you had something to do with his being there?"

Alec nodded. "In a way," he said. "I mean his horse was already in Nassau. I told him it was better to race Flame there than at Hialeah."

"That was good advice," Henry said. "Phantoms aren't what you might call popular with race secretaries in the United States. They seldom live up to their press clippings."

"This one might. At least you just heard what Cornwell said of him on his show."

"That's Cornwell for you," Henry said, chuckling. "He's that kind of a sportscaster, always looking for something spectacular, however fantastic it might be."

"But such a story isn't something a track's publicity department ignores either," Alec said. "Including Hialeah Park."

Henry was silent a moment, then said, "You put

Steve Duncan up to this, didn't you." It was a statement, not a question.

"I didn't know how it would work out," Alec admitted. "He might not have won at Nassau."

"But he did. Why are you doing it, Alec?"

"He needs the money."

"So do lots of people," Henry said.

"He's got to buy an island," Alec went on.

"A what?"

"An island," Alec repeated, feeling a little foolish.

"That's what I thought you said." Henry picked up his evening paper, then put it down again. "Phantom horses and islands are too much for my imagination, if not yours, Alec. It's none of my business what you do off the track, so I guess I shouldn't try to talk you into staying clear of this Steve Duncan and his horse Flame. I just don't want to hear any more about them, understand? I have trouble enough sleeping these nights, let alone dreaming."

"Okay, Henry. I didn't mean to bring it up."

"Then it's finished?"

"Sure," Alec said. But he wondered if it might not be just the beginning.

The night breeze blew softly off Biscayne Bay in Miami, slowly wafting over crowded streets and rustling the limp fronds of the palm trees. It stirred the papers and debris in gutters, spiraling them into small swirling heaps.

Willy Walsh glanced skyward at the red light blinking on top of the television tower and told Alec, "I get all sick inside when I have to go on television."

Alec smiled. It was a miracle that Willy was there at all after his race of the day before. Nothing should scare him after that!

"What gets me," Willy went on, "is that these TV guys usually think we've got the best racket there is. I mean they think that ten percent of the winner's purse is a good livin'. All I got to say is, if that's so, it's a hard way to make an easy livin'."

"Then tell Cornwell so," Alec said.

"I will, all right." Willy gave his colorful checkered cap a hard tug as if to lend added emphasis to his remark. He shook the sweat from his forehead and mumbled something about the heat and lack of a good wind and the smell of the city.

Looking up at the tall white concrete building they were approaching, Alec said, "There's nothing wrong in being determined about anything you want to say, Willy, just as long as it isn't *blind* determination."

"I know," Willy answered. "I'm not goin' to argue with Cornwell none, no more than I'd punch bigger people than me in the nose. It ain't smart. You end up with a broken head."

Like horses, too, Alec thought. You don't argue with them either. They could get mad in a hurry and show a man how small he was.

Willy reached into his shirt pocket and pulled out a package of peanut-butter crackers. "Want some?" he asked.

Alec nodded and noted the other's hands. They were strong, thick and calloused, yet they undid the small, tightly wrapped package with quick skill. Alec took one of the crackers Willy solemnly offered him, more to be agreeable than because he was hungry. Willy liked to munch. He was always nibbling on something, yet it never seemed to affect his weight. He could ride at 110 pounds and never have any trouble making it. That was because he was small.

Alec said, "It's a good thing neither of us has to worry about making weight, Willy." He spoke matter-of-factly, as one professional to another.

Willy laughed. "You'll never have to worry making weight on the Black, that's for sure. Most of the horses I ride get in a race light. I never had a big horse like him carrying top weight. Yet I've made a good livin' at this game. I can't complain. I'm happy, and maybe someday . . ."

"That chestnut you rode yesterday looks like he might come along," Alec said.

"Puttin' blinkers on him next time might do it," Willy said thoughtfully. "I thought he'd really fly yesterday. But the only direction he flew was backward!" He pushed up his checkered cap and added, "What really matters is that he came out of the race all right." Then, as an afterthought, "Me, too."

"God was with you."

"So were you," Willy said. "But you're right; I did a lot of praying in a fraction of a second." He paused, thinking of the race, then added, "If I'd gone down, not a hoof would've missed me. The whole field would've tossed me around like a rubber ball."

He peered at Alec from beneath his heavy brows and a little smile crossed his face. "Anyway," he said, "it wasn't much of a race for you and the Black. We were like a bunch of dogs chasing a bunny."

As they entered the building, Willy tipped his cap over one eye again, partially hiding his face. His voice came from beneath the peak. "I wish I could get out of this. Like I said, it makes me feel sick inside."

The television studio was air-conditioned, its large windows overlooking the gaudy pattern of Miami lights and the causeways stretching across the bay beach areas.

Count Cornwell, whom Alec never had met before, put his cigar down in an ashtray on his desk and came forward to meet them. Smiling, he extended a big hand and said, "Hello, Alec Ramsay. And, of course, Willy Walsh. I'm glad you both could come."

Willy removed his cap self-consciously and Alec studied the tall, stooping man whose head was completely bald. Cornwell was one of the best sportscasters in the business, but you'd never know it to look at him. His expression, at the moment, was bored and vacant, even uninterested. All that would change when he went on the air. He worked hard for a living, and knew everything there was to know about racing.

The telephone on his desk rang and he excused himself to answer it. He smoked as he talked, the smell of his cigar filling the room. When he had replaced the receiver, he leafed quickly through a script on his desk, made a few notes, then heaved himself up from his chair and crossed the room again.

"That's all," he said brusquely. "We're set to go now." He straightened the jacket of his dark suit, adjusted his tie and added, "The others are in the next studio."

Alec followed Cornwell but Willy hung back. "C'mon, Willy," Alec said. "This show is his responsibility, not ours. Let him do the worrying. We're just guests."

"It's too much to ask of anybody," Willy answered, but he followed Alec into the adjoining studio. Four other jockeys were there, sitting in chairs placed in a semicircle around a desk. A battery of lights were winking in the control booth beyond and several men sat before the large board. One man held up three fingers to Cornwell, who glanced at the large clock over the glass-walled booth and nodded in reply.

"Three minutes to air time," he told Alec. "You and Willy take the empty chairs." He went to the desk and sat down, picking up the script and studying it. Then he looked at the group of small men sitting on either side of him. They all seemed to be uncomfortable under the glare of the lights.

"We're checking the line-up of the cameras," Cornwell told them. He glanced at the sweep hand on the large clock again, then at the monitors below the control booth. He studied his own image as it appeared on the monitor, then his guests'. They all looked like what they were, horsebackers. It should be a good show. His mouth widened into a large, friendly smile as the program director's hand swept down and the light on Camera One blinked red. He was on the air.

"Good evening, fellow Miamians, this is 'Count' Cornwell. . . ."

Alec scarcely listened. He was not much interested in the brief account of the day's sports activities which

Cornwell was giving prior to his interview with the riders. Anyway, except for Cornwell they were all off camera and had several minutes to themselves before going on the air. Alec stole a look at the other jockeys to see how they were taking it.

Willy Walsh was still scared by it all but he seemed to have got hold of himself. Jay Pratt, shorter than Willy, was in the next chair; he was wearing a buff-colored turtleneck sweater under a sports jacket. He looked clean and natty, giving evidence of the money he made racing. Jay never worked horses in the mornings any more. He got up just in time to go to the track for the afternoon program. One could do that when owners and trainers started running after you with the big-stake mounts.

Pete Edge sat alongside Jay, his short legs crossed. He was built square and was strong enough to drag the carcass of a dead horse out of his stall, which Alec had seen him do. His left eyelid drooped slightly and a long scar ran directly beneath it, the result of a bad fall and steel-shod hoofs. It made him look tough, which he was, and unhappy, which he also was. He hadn't been winning many races lately.

Gustavo Carballido, one of the very successful South American riders at the present Hialeah meeting, sat in the next chair. As usual, Gus needed a haircut. His dark skin was stretched drum-tight across his cheekbones, making hs eyes seem all the more sunken and piercing. He looked ravaged and hungry despite his current success on the track. There was no doubt that the lean, poverty-stricken years he had known on his way to the top had left their mark.

Next to him was Nick Marchione, the oldest rider at Hialeah, who listed his age as "39 going on 60." He was one of the great jockeys of all time and would probably never retire so long as he continued winning races. He squinted through glasses, which he never wore when riding, and watched Cornwell do his sportscast, and kept running his fingertips through his thinning hair.

Alec's gaze shifted back to Willy Walsh, who was young and inexperienced compared to the others. Willy was rubbing a large gold ring on his left hand. It was, Alec knew, supposed to bring him good luck. Most horsemen were superstitious, Alec reflected. They believed in all manner of charms and taboos for good and bad luck, and every kind of cure-all. Willy had his ring. Jay Pratt wore a medallion with the figure of a bird in flight around his neck. Henry carried horse chestnuts in his pocket. And, Alec admitted, he himself had a silver dollar he'd never be without.

Cornwell was coming to the end of his résumé of the day's sports news. Putting down his script, he fingered his immaculate tie and ran his hand softly over the top of his bald head. Through Camera One he beamed at the riders who sat around the desk. At the same time, his eyes were very probing.

Alec prepared himself for what was to come. He felt his muscles tense, almost as if he were in the starting gate, waiting for the doors to open. And he knew it was no different for the other riders.

Men Without Horses

9

"And now," Cornwell told his television audience, "I want you to meet some of America's greatest jockeys." He introduced them with Camera Two singling out each rider as he spoke. He thought how unlike other athletes they were, these men of the saddle. They sat uncomfortably in their chairs, looking very drawn and stringy despite their well-cut clothes. A couple of them might even be taken for emaciated children. Yet their muscle-banded shoulders and forearms could guide and control a thousand pounds of tough horse running some forty miles an hour. Marchione and Carballido looked harder and more used than the others, as if their lean bodies had endured so much that physical resilience was wearing thin.

He concluded his introductions with Willy Walsh and Alec Ramsay. How young-looking they were! How many more rides before they looked like the others? How many more spills, when all of a sudden a horse went out from under them like a tree limb breaking, and they were down among the sharp hoofs? Thinking of it made Cornwell realize how glad he was not to be one of them. They weren't paid too much even if they made a thousand dollars a day, he decided.

"And now," he told his audience, "we'll talk to these crack jockeys one at a time, starting with the oldest and the country's best-known veteran campaigner, Nick Marchione. Nick," he said pointedly, "you've been riding racehorses for over thirty years now. Don't you think it's time you packed your trunk and left the jockey room?"

Nick Marchione did not appear to be taken aback by Cornwell's directness or sharpness of tongue. His image alone was on the screen of the monitor. He seemed delighted to be there. His lined face was excited, even impatient, as if he were overflowing with new ideas which he wanted to divulge to the vast television audience.

"I'll quit only when I can't give my best . . . that's the only way I ride," he said cockily. "How else would you want me to put it?"

"Then you feel you can still do full justice to your mounts?" Cornwell asked.

"I wouldn't be here if I didn't. I have a responsibility to the people I ride for and the racing public."

"You find that your eyes don't bother you? I'd heard you had some trouble with them."

Marchione shrugged his shoulders and, at the same time, squinted through his glasses. "I wouldn't say they don't bother me none, but not enough to affect my riding. I'm near-sighted, so all I been doin' for the last few years is to stay closer to the pace whenever possible."

"And when you can't? Or say there's a heavy fog or

storm?" Cornwell persisted cagily.

"I use my ears. I'm not deaf. I can tell where I am, all right," Marchione answered, grinning into the camera.

"Is competition tougher these days . . . I mean than it was, say, ten or fifteen years ago?" Cornwell asked.

"No, it's always been tough, like any competitive sport. Jockeys love to beat one another, regardless of the importance of the race. I mean, the size of the purse isn't as important to me as you probably think it is. I get as much kick out of bringing home a winner as I ever did."

"The daily grind doesn't bother you?"

"What daily grind?" Marchione asked. "For me there *is* no daily grind. I love horses and racing. I like to ride. I don't want to do anything else."

"Then you'll only hang up your silks when you feel you can no longer give your best?"

"That's right. As long as I'm physically able to ride, I'll ride."

"You've had plenty of spills?"

"Plenty. I was even pronounced dead after a race on a Midwest half-miler about fifteen years ago."

"Fortunately for you, the diagnosis proved incorrect," Cornwell said, smiling.

"Yeah, fortunately," Marchione repeated solemnly. "And I won the race as well. I crossed the finish wire with my feet in the air and my head beneath the horse before I hit the dirt."

"You sound as if you'd pay to ride if you had to," Cornwell said.

"I might at that," Marchione answered.

"What advice, if any, do you have for young riders on their way up?"

Marchione said hesitantly, "When you're green you can make a million mistakes. Lots of situations come up that kids can't handle. What I tell them is try not to get discouraged. As you get older you learn never to give up hope or quit trying. Among the biggest thrills I've had was winning races where I never thought I had a chance."

"Do you find that young riders listen to you?"

"No. There's nobody smarter than a seventeen-year-old kid." He glanced at Willy Walsh and smiled. "I know, because I was just as stubborn at their age. Now I find I'm doing the same things the old riders told me to do. It's too late to thank most of them."

The camera, shifting quickly to Willy Walsh, showed him sitting on the edge of his chair, listening to Nick Marchione's sage advice.

"Willy," Cornwell said, as if all this had been prearranged, "you're seventeen years old. How do you feel about what Nick just said?"

"I listen to everybody. I always listen," Willy said, shifting uncomfortably in his seat and wishing it were a saddle instead. "But like Nick said, you can make a million mistakes and some of 'em aren't even in the book yet. A lot of things happen in horse racing that can't be explained by nobody, even old guys like Nick."

"What do you weigh, Willy?"

"Generally around one hundred and four pounds

stripped. With rigging an added six pounds, I can ride at a hundred and ten."

"Does the rigging include the safety helmet you jocks wear?"

"No. They let us step on the scales without the helmet. It's a good thing."

"Why?"

"The new helmets weigh about a pound and a half. That much added to tack would put a lot of jocks in a steam box."

"A pound and a half," Cornwell repeated. "That's a lot of weight to be carrying on top of your head during a race."

"Yeah, but it's good to have there in case you go down. It's saved a lot of lives already."

"I imagine it has," Cornwell said. He paused before going on. "Willy, are you a sentimentalist like Nick here? I mean, do you love riding so much you'd stay in this sport whether you were successful or not?"

"Sure I would," Willy said quickly, "if anybody would have me. We all would or we wouldn't be here."

"Not I," Jay Pratt interrupted, and the camera switched to where he sat comfortably in his chair, exuding poise and self-confidence.

"You wouldn't?" Cornwell asked. "Why not?"

"It's a business," Pratt said, his blue eyes laughing, "not a sport. No one ever told me I had to love horses to be in it. I make decisions every day, just like you do in your business or any other executive. I decide where I want to race and what horses I want to ride. I leave the exercising and training and loving to others."

Cornwell smiled back at the handsome jockey in the natty-looking sweater and sports jacket. "I've heard that you get up just in time to make the afternoon races," he said.

"There's nothing wrong with that. Many of the top trainers believe in strong, heavy exercise boys being up on their horses in the morning. It helps to get a horse dead fit in his training."

"And lets you get more sleep," Cornwell suggested.

"Why not? I've been at this business a long time, almost as long as Nick here."

"What do you think is the most important quality a rider can have?"

"Confidence is the big thing. Like I just said, I make a lot of decisions every day, and I can't afford to hesitate. I've learned to act quickly and confidently. When I decide to move with a horse, we move, inside or outside. I don't change my mind once we're on our way. I decide before I move how much horse I got under me and whether or not I can make it, then I go."

"And if you've made the wrong decision?" Cornwell asked.

"I get in a jam like anyone else. But I don't make many wrong moves any more. I keep my horse free of trouble and going all the time."

"Have you been around horses since you were a kid, Jay?" Cornwell asked.

"No. I was born and brought up in New York City. The only horses I saw were the cops' horses in the streets and a few that hacked around Central Park."

"Then why were you attracted to racing?"

"I wanted to get to Florida for the winter months," Jay Pratt said, laughing. "So I went to the racetrack and learned to ride."

The camera switched to the man in the next chair, and Cornwell said, "Here's another rider who has had to work hard to get where he is . . . Pete Edge."

"We all know what it is to work hard," Pete said, looking fierce because of his drooping eyelid and scar. "The difference is that only a few are making money at it."

Cornwell smiled. "It's true you've had a run of hard luck at Hialeah this season, Pete. How do you account for it?"

"You get a lot of bad horses, like I have, and they make you look like a bum. It's as simple as that."

"You were brought up in the city, too, weren't you, Pete?"

"Chicago. Like Jay here, all I knew about horses at first was that one end bit and the other end kicked. Then I went to the track mornings and found I could stick on 'em."

"Do you still exercise horses in the mornings?"

"Sure. I don't have any choice like Jay does, but I'd do it anyway. I keep fit by working. I feel as good now as I did when I was Willy's age. I don't drink or smoke and I got a wife who understands."

"That helps," Cornwell said, smiling and thinking how incongruous it was for this rider with the tough, scarred face to be talking about living the clean life. But there was no doubt that Pete Edge was strong on fortitude.

"Everyone has a run of hard luck once in a while," Cornwell went on. "I'm sure you'll have a successful comeback."

"I hope so, but I can't ride any faster than a horse can run," Pete Edge said, smiling. "Most of those I been riding here eat so much dust I think of them as equine vacuum cleaners."

"But you're always in there trying, Pete. No one uses a whip more than you do."

"That's not so," the rider said angrily. "I don't use a bat more than any other rider. I got the reputation for makin' more use of it because I swing in a wide arc, hitting my horses more on the rump than the flanks. It can be seen easy from the stands but I do it because it hurts a horse less than whipping on the side and gets the job done just as well. It gives me a chance to use my whip in close quarters, too, and stay in rhythm with my horse's strides."

"I see," Cornwell said, although he didn't. "And now," he continued, "we'll talk to Gustavo Carballido, one of the brightest stars to come out of the Argentine in a long time. Gus," he asked, "how do you account for the large number of riders who are coming up from South America and the West Indies and are racing so successfully?"

The dark eyes flashed. "The good riders, like the good horses, come from anywhere," Gustavo said slowly, carefully selecting his words.

"What is the greatest trouble you foreign riders have?" Cornwell asked.

"Learning English so we can understand the orders from trainers," Gustavo answered, smiling.

"It's no secret that many of our nation's top grass races, including the Hialeah Turf Cup, which is coming up soon, have been very profitable affairs for foreign-bred entries. How do you account for that, Gustavo?"

"The South American trainer, he is a good horseman and he develops a horse well. It is also summer in South America now and horses are very, very good."

"So these South American trainers consider it worthwhile to fly themselves and their horses north for a shot at valuable races. Is that right, Gustavo?"

"That is right, I think. Many are here. I ride one today."

"And you won?"

"No. He no have it. I try to go inside with him, but he no go. The hole she close and I take him up or I go down. I get helpless feeling inside." He put a small hand on his stomach. "I cross my fingers and say a prayer. He stay up and we finish, but not very good. He no like the dirt. Next time we go on the grass and he do better, much better. You will see."

"I will see," Cornwell repeated. "Yes, I know that some horses who race well over dirt can't do the same on grass—and vice versa. For a while the top trainers in the United States were reluctant to race their horses over turf, but that attitude is fast disappearing. Grass racing is a beautiful spectacle and, of course, it's the only kind of racing in South America and Europe. If our champions are to meet foreign champions, it must be done on grass. Besides, there's no doubt that the international aspect of any race always increases its popularity."

Glancing at Alec Ramsay, Cornwell went on, "Yesterday the Black proved his grass-racing ability by winning in record time. What did you think of him, Gustavo? How does he compare with the champions of South America?"

"I no see him run," Gustavo said. "It is important for me to see him run before I say."

Cornwell said, "You must be one of the very few, Gus, who have never seen the Black race. Television has made him one of the best-known horses in the world and his racing record is just about perfect. His time yesterday over a turf course softened by heavy rains was remarkable. For two years now he's been the U.S. 'Horse of the Year' and it seems he is well on his way to earning an unprecedented third championship. Let's talk to his pilot, Alec Ramsay."

The camera shifted and Alec, seeing his image on the monitor screen, became uneasy. He was glad when Cornwell went on talking after a few seconds' pause.

"Alec," Cornwell said, "there aren't many horsemen who could bring back a champion after a long lay-up and have him ready for a race like the one the Black ran yesterday. Don't you agree?"

"Henry Dailey has a master's touch when it comes to conditioning a horse," Alec answered.

"Now that the Black has returned to the races, have you any worries about his campaign for capturing another national title?"

"I'm worried," Alec admitted, "but it's nice to have such worries. They put a hundred and thirty-six pounds on him yesterday, so I'm wondering what it will be in the ones coming up."

"You mean there's a point beyond which he can't go?"

"Sure, and we don't know where it is," Alec said.

"Grass racing must be easier on his injured foot," Cornwell suggested.

"His foot's okay," Alec answered. "For a while Henry had him working in a shoe with a thick leather pad. He didn't want any dirt or sand to work into the sore spot and cause more trouble. But he took off the pad a few weeks ago and replaced it with a wafer-thin piece of leather that seems to be doing the job."

"It looked that way yesterday," Cornwell agreed.

"He's just 'coming up' now after not racing so long. He'll do still better next time out."

Cornwell studied the crimson-haired youth. "How's you own thoroughbred breeding venture coming along, Alec?"

"It's coming," Alec said pleasantly. "It's too early to say any more about it."

"I hear you've got some colts and fillies up at Hopeful Farm that are better than many of the youngsters racing here."

"That remains to be seen," Alec said. "We don't intend to start any of them before next year."

Cornwell nodded. In Alec Ramsay he saw a very serious horseman who was poised and articulate before the cameras. He appeared to be as comfortable on television as he was on a horse's back. He should be around racing a long time, and would probably break every record in the book before he was done—that is, unless Henry Dailey pushed him too hard. Henry was the dynamo behind this quiet but determined Alec Ramsay.

"Then you and Henry Dailey were satisfied with the Black's race yesterday?" Cornwell asked.

"Of course," Alec said. "He ran a game race all the way. He was in close quarters at first and pulled clear when I asked him to."

"Then you won't have any excuses for him in the races coming up? You believe he's in the full bloom of his career, ready to meet any contender for his title?"

"I can't say we won't have any excuses if he's beaten," Alec said. "But he won't permit himself to be beaten without some good reason for it."

"I suppose you're right. He has a lot of courage. I've seen him come from far back and still win."

"It takes more courage for a horse to lead all the way and turn back horses that come at him in the stretch," Alec said. "That's a lot tougher than running past the other horses."

"Perhaps you're right."

"But the Black is happy either way. It doesn't make any difference to him which way we decide to run the race."

"Happy?" Cornwell smiled wryly. "Is that what you said?"

"Yes," Alec said, "my horse is happy. If a horse isn't happy he won't run for you."

"But as you said earlier, weight might stop him one of these days," Cornwell commented. "To me, it doesn't seem fair that great horses should be heavily handicapped so other horses can beat them."

Nick Marchione spoke up quickly. "I hate to

interrupt," he said, "but you'd better get hold of a dictionary and look up the word 'handicap,' Mr. Cornwell."

The camera switched to the veteran jockey with the gray, thinning hair and spectacles.

"It means the same now as it always did," Nick went on. "A handicap is a race in which, in order to equalize chances of winning, a disadvantage of carrying more weight is given to a competitor of recognized superiority. If a champion like the Black isn't up to carrying the weight assigned to him, he shouldn't be entered in handicaps."

"That's true, of course," Cornwell said. "But the point Alec Ramsay is making, I believe, is that there's a limit to what his horse can carry without the risk of breaking down. Is that right, Alec?"

"Yes. You put a lot of weight on a horse racing over a long distance and he might break down in the stretch..A tired horse is always more prone to injury."

"It depends upon the type of horse," Nick Marchione said. "If he's big and rugged and trained right, he can carry up to a hundred and sixty pounds safely. I've seen great horses carry as much as that."

"A trainer is just asking for trouble if he allows it," Alec said.

Nick smiled into the camera. "You mean it just gives a trainer an excuse for some other trouble he's having with his horse, and not the high weight that's on his back. I been around a long time, Alec. I know."

Cornwell interrupted. "I still think a track should limit the amount of weight put on a great horse's back."

"When a racetrack limits the weight put on 'name' horses like the Black," Nick explained, "it usually does it to attract them to the race and therefore attract more people to the stands. But when that's done it's not a *true* handicap. That's all I'm driving at."

Cornwell said, "I doubt that's done very often, Nick. But I certainly feel there should be a weight ceiling for superior horses. No one wants to see them break down."

"Then they shouldn't be racing in handicaps," Nick persisted. "Not if the trainer feels his horse is going to break down under the weight assigned. That's all I mean. A real standout horse that comes along every so often should be able to carry high weights. I've seen a few do it. That's what has made them great."

Alec said nothing.

Willy Walsh spoke up. "All I got to say after yesterday's race," he said quietly, "is that the Black *is* one of the great horses of all time. He scares me when I see him run. He just plain scares me, that's all."

Jay Pratt grinned. "Maybe the rest of us don't scare so easy, Willy," he said. "Like Nick said, a big weight shift onto a horse can make a race mighty interesting."

"It won't bother the Black much," Willy said. "He's just better than any other horse we got around here. I don't think he'll be beaten. But there's always second money every time I go up against him, and that buys a lot of hay. That's the way I look at it."

"Maybe the best horse won't win the next time the Black goes out," Pete Edge said. "Lady Luck always plays a part in horse racing. I like a rider who can win on the second-best horse once in a while."

Cornwell glanced at the large clock over the glass-walled booth and nodded to his director. It was time to inject his final comments, and he always liked to conclude his show in the most dramatic way possible.

"Well, anyway you look at it," he said, "the publicity thumpers at Hialeah Park never had it so good. The large host of winter visitors here in Miami have the privilege of seeing the famous Black in the full bloom of his career; this alone will account for many extra thousands of fans turning out every time he runs. The news of his racing over the infield course will heighten interest in the international aspect of the coming Hialeah Turf Cup."

He paused, and then continued, "And a separate, tasty morsel served up on a silver platter is yesterday's news from Nassau. The island horse Flame won the Nassau Cup in the same record-breaking time as the Black at Hialeah. However unique Nassau horse racing may be, Flame's performance is worthy of attention. We suggest that it would be excellent public relations for Hialeah to extend an invitation to this horse to come here to race the Black. And now, thank you, gentlemen, for coming . . . and good night, all."

The camera shifted to the riders and the show ended.

Flame

10

Two evenings after the television show Alec received a phone call and hurriedly left Hialeah Park. He caught a bus which took him the short distance to Miami International Airport, where Steve Duncan and his horse Flame awaited him.

Intentionally, he had not called Henry at his motel, knowing full well that the old trainer would object to his going anywhere to meet Steve and what Henry continued to call a "phantom" horse. Glancing out the bus window, Alec saw the lights of a huge plane making its landing at the airport. Steve had said on the telephone that he had arrived three days ago, immediately following his race in Nassau. Flame was being held in quarantine by the Department of Agriculture, pending health tests and settlement of his racing status in the United States.

Alec felt confident that Flame would be allowed to race at Hialeah. The vacation dollar was as important to Florida as it was to Nassau, and Hialeah's press agentry would not miss this opportunity to boost the track and the state's economy by inviting the Bahamian champion to race. Contrary to what Henry had said, phantom horses did not break records every year

126

and people would turn out to see them run. Flame was made to order for Hialeah's press department. He could be one of the young year's greatest attractions.

Alec settled back in his bus seat. Good horses could come from anywhere, and within a short time he'd see Flame and know more about him. But it was one thing for a horse to be invincible racing against native, island-bred horses and something else to compete against those racing at Hialeah Park. It took more than brilliant speed, providing Flame *did* possess it, to win at a major track. The speed had to be turned on and off, used when it would be most effective to get a position and keep out of trouble. And trouble could be a decisive factor in any big race.

Alec rode the bus to the end of the field where the hangars and offices of the cargo airlines were located. He watched the signs for the name of Air Caribbean, the airline that had brought Steve Duncan and Flame to Miami. He had never heard of it before.

But then he knew few of the cargo airlines which the bus passed so quickly—Air International, Real, Tan, Aaxico, Seminole, Aerocondor, Lebia International, Rutas and many others. Most of them flew cargo to South America, Central America and the West Indies. There were trailer trucks everywhere and huge areas filled with cargo planes for sale. It was a far different world from the glistening passenger terminal on the other side of the airport.

Finally Alec saw the sign, Air Caribbean, and left the bus. He walked up the road toward the hangars, his pace quickening at the prospect of seeing Flame. He recalled how similar this night was to one he had known long ago. He, too, had arrived in the United States with a strange "phantom" horse capable of a speed no one would have believed.

He approached the office at the far end of a large shed. Before reaching the door he heard his name called and Steve Duncan stepped out of the doorway. Startled, Alec took a step backward. "I must be nervous tonight," he said jokingly.

"You and me both," Steve answered. "I never expected to get this far with him. I mean, I'd hoped to race him here but I didn't figure on it. It makes me jumpy just thinking about it."

Alec said, "You're bound to be jumpy. Waiting around for a race is always the worst. You must have played plenty of sports. You should know how it is."

"No, I don't know. I never played much of anything. I was always too light to make any of the teams. They always made me the towel boy or the manager." Steve laughed, easing his tenseness somewhat. "I've handled more towels than horses. I can tell you that much."

"Maybe you do a better job with horses than with towels," Alec said.

"Maybe so." Steve's face continued working nervously and there was a wariness in his eyes.

"How come you're so worried about him? You weren't the first time we met," Alec reminded him. "You were pretty cocky."

"Not worried, just nervous . . . like I said. Maybe he won't run his race. Maybe the long trip and the change will affect him."

"Usually a horse runs his best race the first time out

after a long trip," Alec said. "Say five or six days after
he arrives. It's only after that when changes in
climate, water and such things may affect him. He
ought to run his race if you get him in soon."

"I hope so." Steve moved toward the doors of the
shed and Alec followed. "Pitch is here, too," he said.
"I want you to meet him."

"How long will they keep Flame here?" Alec asked.

"The Department veterinarian took a blood test
when we arrived and we got an okay on it this
afternoon. That's why I called you."

"You're clear to go, then?"

Steve nodded. "For racing purposes only, providing
Hialeah will have us."

"Did you contact the track?" Alec asked.

"Yesterday. They want to see him work first. They
want to be sure."

Alec smiled. "Then what are you worrying about? If
he's all you say he is . . ."

"See for yourself," Steve said, opening the door of
the shed. The building, brightly lit, was a bedlam of
bawling, chattering animals in pens and cages.

Alec followed Steve inside, listening to the sounds
and identifying those from donkeys, parrots, monkeys
and parakeets. There were many animals and birds
from the islands and South America with which he was
unfamiliar, all bound for zoos and new homes in the
United States.

A slightly built man came down the corridor to meet
them and Steve said, "This is my friend Pitch. Phil
Pitcher."

Alec shook Pitch's hand, wondering if the man

really felt as sad as he looked. There seemed to be worry, too, in the eyes that peered at him from behind steel-rimmed glasses. His soft, round face was deeply tanned but expressionless, his hair brown with no trace of gray. He wore knee-length shorts and held a straw sun hat in one hand, a combination—the shorts especially, attracting attention as they did to his knobby knees—which made him look a little ridiculous.

Pitch removed his limp hand from Alec's but still peered shortsightedly at him. "Steve told me you were coming," he said quietly; his voice was tired. "He seemed to think you might help . . ."

Alec wanted to say something to alleviate the misery and worry in the man's eyes. "I don't know just what Steve wants me to do, but I'll help if I can. It's pretty much up to your horse."

"Yes . . . yes, I know. I'm quite aware of that. He's . . . well, come and see for yourself."

There was a pause and an exchange of glances between Pitch and Steve. Then the man slipped back the bolt on a closed stall.

With the sliding of the bolt came the whinny of a stallion. Alec felt his muscles grow tense. No domesticated horse ever made quite that sound. It was the whinny of a wild stallion, and it faded to a few whiffling snorts when Steve entered the stall.

Alec would have followed but Pitch had placed a restraining hand on his arm.

"Isn't it safe to go in?" Alec asked.

"Oh, it's safe, all right," Pitch answered seriously. "Steve works miracles. At least it seems so to me. I'm not much with horses. In fact, I know very little about them. And the more I'm around Flame, the more I realize how much I have to learn."

"It takes time," Alec said, "and nothing can take the place of experience."

"I'm really not very much interested in horses at all," Pitch confessed, actually looking bored. "I have my own work to do. You see, I'm a historian . . . I dabble a bit in archaeology, too."

"I see," Alec said. But he decided that Pitch's bored air was completely false and that he was failing miserably in trying to convince his listener that he wasn't interested in Flame.

"Then why are you here?" Alec asked.

"To do what I can to help, of course," Pitch answered. "As I say, I'm not much good with Flame but I do act as Steve's bookkeeper . . . or a better name for it might be his racing accountant. We have seven hundred ninety-eight dollars and sixty-three cents at the present time. Our expenses getting here were heavy, but Steve says I can expect another check soon, a big one."

Alec noted the gleam in the blue eyes behind the steel-rimmed glasses but said nothing. He didn't want to disillusion Pitch by telling him that winning a race at Hialeah wasn't as easy as winning one at Nassau.

Steve called to them and they entered the stall.

Flame was not what Alec had expected. He had anticipated seeing a small horse, like most of the horses from the islands, with just a streak of wildness in him. But as he looked upon Flame, standing against the rear wall of his stall, it was as if he had always known this horse. Flame had come from the same mold as the Black.

The stallion's defiant gaze was centered on Alec; his wedge-shaped head was turned slightly to the side, and his small ears were pricked forward. He was as large as the Black and as finely made, from the well-muscled withers, chest and shoulders to the unusually long quarters and strong legs. His coat, of course, was altogether different—a glowing, red chestnut that made one think of fire.

Alec looked at him for a long time, not knowing or caring if the two other persons there spoke to him or not. *There could not in this whole world be another horse so like my own,* he thought. *Henry said they broke the mold after the Black. I have said it. Time and time again I have said it . . . and believed it.*

But he and Henry had been wrong. The mold had *not* been broken. This horse had the same arrogance and stamp of nobility as the Black. And Flame continued to regard him much as a king might have done in granting one of his subjects an audience.

Alec listened as Steve talked to Flame in unintelligible murmurings accompanied by soft, gentle touches. It was a language that belonged solely to Steve and Flame, yet Alec recognized it for what it was. It was not unlike the way he and the Black communicated.

Flame lowered his head at the bidding of the boy beside him. Steve straightened the silky foretop that had dropped over his eyes and smoothed the mane which was too long and heavy for a groomed racehorse. Alec now believed everything Steve had told

him about Flame and his island, wherever it was. He
noted several jagged scars on Flame's body, scars that
could only have been the result of battle with other
stallions.

Suddenly Alec decided that he wanted to know
nothing more than he already did about this horse and
his master. The less he knew, the less he would
become involved in Steve's world, whatever and
wherever it was. He had the Black, and that left no
time for anything else.

Just then Steve turned to him and said, "The only
trouble I had with him in Nassau was when I needed
to take him away from the crowd to be saddled. Other
than that he was okay."

"He looks like the kind you can't fool around with
much," Alec said.

"He's fine as long as I don't take hold of him and try
to take him back. He wants to run too much."

"No horse can go full speed all the way," Alec said.
"Even with one that's always running and trying,
you've got to give him a breather somewhere."

"Not Flame. He doesn't know where the end is. He
just keeps going. You've never seen a horse like this
one, Alec."

Alec turned away from Steve's beaming face and
tried hard not to resent the youth's confidence in his
horse. There was a day not so long ago when he
himself had talked the very same way about the Black.
No one had listened to him or believed him until the
Black had raced.

"It's always hard to estimate a horse's chances

before you see him run," Alec said. "But he looks real good."

Pitch reached into his pocket and drew out a short pipe, regarding Alec intently as he filled it. "I understand from what Steve has told me that you're no youngster when it comes to horses. I respect your advice, as I'm sure Steve does. But although I know nothing about this business of racing horses, there are certain things I've observed. One of them, and the most important at this moment, is that no horse could possibly run as fast as Flame. All he has to do to win is simply get in a big race and avoid . . . uh, trouble."

Alec shrugged his shoulders. "Avoiding trouble is part of racing," he said quietly. "We all try to keep our horses clear and give them a chance to run their race. That will be Steve's job, too." He turned to the boy. "Even if you do happen to have the fastest horse in the world, no jockey is going to make it easy for you to win."

Pitch put his filled pipe back in his pocket, and took a deep breath. "I understand, Alec," he said, "and I want you to know that we'll be good sports. But we came here to make money. We must leave with it."

Alec smiled. "That's why everybody's here. You're not alone."

Pitch squinted through his glasses and scratched his head. Then he sighed. "Yes, I suppose you're right. Everybody needs money these days. It's a terrible strain."

"But not everybody needs it quite as fast as you do, or needs quite so much. Sixty-five thousand dollars is a lot of money for a horse to earn."

Pitch glanced at Steve, then back at Alec. "Then he's told you?"

"That you need that much money to buy your island? Yes. Steve told me that."

The man shrugged his shoulders. "Racing Flame was the only way we could think of to get it."

Alec, looking at Flame again, said, "It might be possible, providing you give him and yourselves enough time. Even with the high purses we have today, it's tough to get in the money. It takes not only a fast horse but lots of experience . . . and neither Flame nor Steve have had any except for the Nassau race."

Steve said cockily, "They still pay off on the first horse around the track, Alec."

"Yes, they do," Alec agreed. He studied Steve's face a moment and then asked, "When will you move him to the track?"

"I promised to work him tomorrow morning. If they like him, we'll be able to race him in the Hialeah Turf Cup. That's worth about seventy thousand dollars to the winner. It's all we need. We could pack up and go home."

"You'd have the Black to beat, you know," Alec reminded him.

"I know."

"It doesn't bother you?"

"No, not really," Steve said. "I don't mean I wouldn't like to avoid the Black right now, but we don't have time to wait."

"That's what you said before." Alec started toward the door. "Well, I'll see you at the track tomorrow morning then."

"Alec . . ."

"Yes?"

"Will you be working the Black tomorrow? I mean . . . if you are, do you think you could work him with us?"

"Together? The Black and Flame?"

"Yes. You see . . . what I mean is that it would impress the track officials more than if I worked Flame alone. They'd see the kind of horse he is when he could stay with the Black."

Alec met the other's gaze. "But what if he doesn't?"

"Oh, he will, all right."

Once again Alec tried hard not to resent Steve's confidence in himself and his horse. He shrugged his shoulders. "Henry calls the shots in the Black's training," he said. "But I do happen to know he's got a work scheduled for tomorrow morning. Maybe we'll be on the track at the same time."

"That's all I want," Steve said. "Just give us a chance to be out there together."

Red and Black

11

On his way to the track the next morning the Black stopped every now and then to follow the antics of squirrels scrambling up and down the tall Australian pines. He pricked up his ears, too, at the sound of the birds' trills.

Alec did not urge him on. Slow walks through Hialeah paths were an important part of the Black's training. Also, they helped relieve the tiredness and boredom which might affect any horse stabled at a racetrack.

Alec glanced in the direction of the busy track, wondering if Steve Duncan and his horse Flame were already there. But they couldn't be, he decided, for Henry would have mentioned it to him; the trainer was sitting in the grandstand with a bunch of old friends and clockers.

Henry had been less interested than Alec had anticipated when he had told of his visit to Steve the previous evening. "If Hialeah wants such a horse here, that's their business," he had said unconcernedly. "As for working him and the Black together, it's a public track. If he's out there the same time we are, I can't stop him from going around."

Alec patted the Black's neck. He wasn't worried about Flame's reported speed. No horse in the world could stay alongside the Black. Yet Alec knew that he was not the only jockey who thought his horse unbeatable. Most riders overestimated their mounts. Every jockey thought he could win on a special horse.

At the gap in the fence, Alec kept the Black on the outside of the track and let him go into a lope to loosen up. The stallion moved effortlessly, giving the impression to everyone who watched that running was wonderfully easy. For him it was.

Alec recalled the days when the Black was strictly a come-from-behind horse. It had taken a lot of racing luck as well as tremendous speed to break through large fields and win. Now the Black could be rated and Alec could take him out in front early if necessary, and place him where he thought racing would be easier for both of them. It helped to keep them out of trouble; and trouble, as he had told Steve last night, could be a decisive factor in any big race.

The Black was pricking up his ears and watching two horses just ahead of him. Even when he was merely loosening up he was looking for horses to beat. With head held high, he coasted between them and went on.

Alec let him go but talked to him softly. "Easy, big fellow," he said.

How long would it be before Steve showed up? he wondered. He knew how the boy felt, for he had gone through the same thing himself. Steve had just won his first race, and for any jockey there was nothing in the world to compare with the feeling the first win

gave you. It remained with you for all time no matter
how successful you became later. You wouldn't trade
it for a million dollars.

Alec recalled how scared he was the first time he'd
raced the Black. He hadn't thought he was ready to
ride, and he might not have ridden at all if Henry
hadn't insisted. He had been so nervous he'd forgotten to pull down his goggles until the dirt started
hitting him in the face. He had closed his eyes and had
just sat in the saddle, letting the Black run his own
race and break through the field to win. It had been a
day he'd never forget.

While all this was running through his mind, Alec
continued galloping the Black the long way around the
main track as Henry had ordered. The old trainer
wanted the Black tough and rugged so he could go a
distance.

"We have a Cup horse," Henry had stated calmly
and firmly. "We will train him as such."

Alec had no doubt that the Black was doing
brilliantly. He had raced a mile easily and had finished
strong. A strong finish was even more important when
the races lengthened.

The Black entered the backstretch and Alec kept
him near the outside rail, leaving room for the
working horses racing past. The Black snorted as they
passed. He would have enjoyed going after them, Alec
knew, but he obeyed his rider. He knew he was there
only to gallop.

Alec leaned forward and pressed his cheek against
the stallion's neck. His horse was truly beautiful but
what Alec appreciated even more was his great

courage, never so manifest as when the breaks went against him in a race. It was then that the Black showed his true greatness.

There would be races they might lose, Alec knew. It all depended on the conditions of the races themselves and the conditions of the horses. And, like human beings, horses had their good days and their bad days.

Alec rode the Black around the far turn and went toward the grandstand where Henry awaited them. He wondered how he and Henry would feel if Steve Duncan's horse *did* beat them. He didn't think it possible unless the Black was really out of sorts on race day, but if it happened, at least it would have been in a good cause. The thought of Steve Duncan's need for money to buy his island made Alec smile. No one else at Hialeah Park needed purse money for such a purpose . . . of that he was certain!

Breaking into the horse racing business took courage even for those who had been closely associated with it for a long time. To try to make large sums of money at it without any previous experience was reckless and foolhardy.

Alec tightened rein, slowing down the Black to a jog as he approached Henry and the group of men sitting in a box opposite the finish line.

One of the clockers nudged Henry and said, "You got nothing to worry about this year, old man. He looks and acts better than he ever did."

Henry grunted and shrugged his shoulders. "If you say so, Charley. I'd like to think you're right."

Another clocker laughed and said, "What's goin' to stop him in his million-dollar parade? The big purse races coming up are his for the asking."

"I wouldn't say that," Henry answered.

"Well, I would," the other shot back. "He's the acknowledged champion and nothing here can touch him. He's had one race to tighten him. He'll go on to win at a mile and a quarter and longer."

"He's crying to run, no doubt about that," still another said. "He's the one horse I've seen that lives up to his publicity build-up. His presence here has had an electrifying effect on everybody."

"Especially Hialeah's press department," the clocker named Charley said, grinning. "Strangely enough they have a tender passion for gate receipts. I guess the Black's the most publicized horse of our time." He turned to Henry. "You've started working him pretty hard, Henry. How come?"

"He's ready for all the steady work I can give him," the old trainer said.

"Aren't you afraid he might leave his race on the training track?"

"I don't care how fast he goes, now that he's ready to go."

"Alec will have trouble holding him this morning. He's full of beans."

"He might at that," Henry agreed, watching his horse.

"The press department's been beating the drums about the galaxy of stars the Black will have to beat in the Hialeah Turf Cup," another said. "But the truth is there's none to equal him . . . the 'Big One,' as they say. He towers over all the others like the Colossus of Rhodes."

"Certainly there's nothing at Hialeah that comes close to him," another agreed.

"You all may be talkin' too early," Henry said uncomfortably, worried by the outspoken optimism of his friends. "He ran a great race the other day but he runs best when he's fresh. He might not do so well the next time out."

A reporter smiled and said, "You know as well as we do, Henry, that your horse is only now coming up to his best form. His race the other day spoke for itself. He burst out between those other horses as if they weren't in the race at all. After the race I spoke to Alec and he confirmed what I'd seen for myself. He could have placed the Black anywhere on the track and then sent him to the front anytime he chose. Since Alec can rate the Black when the horse wants to win so badly, it's good enough for me. Sam's right. Nothing here is going to beat him."

"Alec can think faster than most other jockeys can ride," a clocker said. "He knows when to make the right move at the right time. That's what wins most races."

"Talk don't win races," Henry said, "that's for sure."

"Quit worrying, Henry," a close friend said, chuckling.

"I got plenty to worry about," Henry answered. "You should know it as well as I, Cliff. Winning handicap races is no easy job no matter how it might seem on paper. Handicappers try to weight horses so nobody can win and they usually do a good job of it. I don't like to see a whole lot of weight packed on my horse but I usually get what I deserve. My big worry is that my horse comes back all right. If I get beat, I get beat, that's all."

"That's more than I've heard from most trainers," the reporter said, making a note. "Few trainers think a track handicapper treats them fair."

"I'm not saying I don't gripe like other trainers," Henry explained. "But I feel most of us are inclined to pamper our horses too much these days. The only way to breed and develop good, tough horses able to go a distance and stay is to train them steadily."

"But I heard you've been handling the Black so carefully you've been practically spoon-feeding him," the reporter said.

"I wouldn't go that far," Henry returned, "but you're right. I've been a little careful with him this season because of his foot. He's tight now, though, and a rough horse to work around. Alec forks most of the straw in his stall. I stay clear except to grab a sponge once in a while."

They watched Alec bring the Black to a stop in front of them.

The reporter said, "It must be a little difficult working him alone, Henry. That's the beauty of having a large stable . . . being able to try horses against each other, I mean. The competition helps."

"There's no doubt that it helps," Henry said. "But he works well enough alone." He glanced at the tunnel leading from the paddock to the track, and added, "However, we're not figuring on working him alone this morning. I promised Alec—"

He didn't finish for just then he saw Flame emerging from the tunnel, and the sight so startled him that he forgot everything else.

When Flame saw the Black through the gap in the track fence, he raised his head still higher in order to get a good look at the other stallion.

"In the name of heaven, Henry, who is he?" the reporter asked, following the trainer's gaze.

Henry didn't answer. He just looked at the horse he knew had to be Flame.

The red stallion was arrogant and confident, perfectly proportioned, and right now all his senses were keyed to the utmost. He remained alert but he did not challenge the black stallion. He had learned patience long ago. He was cool and steady in the face of danger, a born leader showing no sign of fear.

The reporter said, "Look at the scars. That horse is a mass of cuts and tooth marks."

The men in the box had all turned to examine the new arrival. They saw a magnificent blood-red horse, motionless now except for the occasional pricking up of his ears and the twitching of his nostrils.

Flame was aware of the words and touches of his rider but he kept his eyes on the other stallion. He was waiting for him to move, to attack. He had full confidence in his own courage and cunning but he was very wary.

"I don't like the looks of this at all," a clocker said nervously. "They're going to fight."

"Just like a TV movie," the reporter remarked with feigned humor, but no one smiled.

They had noticed that the Black had not made a move but that he was breathing hard and trembling. Was that due to his gallop, or to his quickened heartbeat and mounting anger? They shifted their gaze to the red stallion again. Was this racetrack to become an arena for two fighting stallions?

Suddenly, the red stallion moved toward the track, where he saw a set of running horses. He reared skyward, wanting to take off in pursuit, but Steve held him back and rode down the track at a slow jog.

"Now I've seen everything," a clocker said.

"Henry, who is he?" the reporter asked again.

"Ask him," Henry answered, nodding to a track official who was entering their box.

The new arrival found himself the center of attention. "Tell us, Tim, who's the horse?" Henry's friend Cliff asked.

"It's Flame," the official said, "winner of the Nassau Cup."

"You're letting him race *here*?"

"If he can run the way he looks."

"You mean *if* the boy can control him."

"That's part of it. He assured me he could. After all, he's raced him before."

"Who's the boy?"

"Steve Duncan."

"An islander, too?"

"It appears so. Don't fret, Cliff. I'm just here to see what they can do. Because they're strangers doesn't mean they should be thrown out. After all, we've had others here less heralded than these two."

"You're not kidding," Cliff said. "The word's out to all the youngsters in the tropics to take a chance and ride in the U.S. It doesn't seem to matter if they're full-fledged jockeys or apprentices."

"And with good reason," the official pointed out. "A number of them have been quite successful."

"Only one out of every hundred makes it," Cliff answered.

Henry said, "You don't have to worry about this kid's riding." His eyes had never left Steve Duncan and Flame. "And he's got a running horse."

"You think so, Henry?" the official asked. "I must report my recommendations to the front office. There are a lot of problems involved in the racing of foreign horses."

"I know, but permits to race can always be granted," Henry said. "The Russian horses got them for the Laurel International and they're not recognized by the International stud books."

The reporter said, "All that's necessary is an outstanding racing record."

"Scientists may have harnessed the atom but horse breeders haven't as yet harnessed the gene," another commented. "Fast horses can come from anywhere, even from the outer islands."

Henry rose from his seat and went to the rail. "Go seven furlongs with him, Alec," he called, "over the main track. Go handily but don't sizzle."

"What about *him*?" Alec asked, nodding in the direction of Flame.

"Stay clear of him. You wanted them to work together. You decide best how to do it."

The Black sensed the challenge that was coming and broke into a run the moment Alec turned him away from the outside rail. He cut down the distance

between himself and Flame, then tried moving closer.
He felt Alec's hands guiding him away from where he
wanted to go. For a few seconds he refused to
respond, then relented and continued down the
middle of the track. His strides lengthening, his hoofs
scarcely seeming to touch the ground, he drew
alongside the red stallion.

Flame matched strides with him, his hoofs, too,
barely touching the earth. He snorted in anger and
attempted to move closer to the other horse. When
Steve held him in, Flame continued snorting but took
out his anger and frustration in ever-lengthening
leaps. His mane and tail streamed in the wind like
wind-swept fire.

As he approached the first turn Alec knew that the
pace was much faster than Henry had wanted for the
Black. He took another wrap in the reins and glanced
over at Steve Duncan.

Steve caught his eyes. "Come on, Alec!" he yelled.
"I'll race you to the wire. The last guy in buys dinner."

Alec shook his head, but the Black took more rein
from him going into the turn. He knew by his horse's
unyielding demands that somehow he found racing
alongside the red stallion different from anything he
had done before and that he felt hostility toward
Flame. An awareness of possible danger made Alec
uneasy as their speed increased.

They had sped by three furlong poles and Alec tried
to slow down the pace but got no response. His horse
was determined not to be left behind by Flame, and
he would have been had he slackened stride an inch.

The Black had his neck stretched out but his ears were still pricked forward, a sign to Alec that he was not yet going all-out.

Racing down the long backstretch, Alec glanced over at Steve Duncan, who was sitting low and forward in his saddle but with his feet withdrawn from the stirrup irons. Only a person used to riding bareback could sit a running horse that way.

The red stallion ran as if he were being eaten up with his own power. He snorted as the Black moved a half-stride ahead, and Alec saw the dangerous glint in his eyes.

Then Flame sprang forward, drawing even with the Black. He was going all-out now. But the Black was going all-out, too! The two horses could not continue at such a speed much longer, Alec knew. He knew too that neither he nor Steve were any longer a part of this race. They were only witnesses to a savage battle that had been going on since the beginning of time. What would have been natural combat between two competing stallions had given way to the strongest instinct of all, *flight*! They would not stop until they had run themselves into the ground.

The reins cut deeply into Alec's wrists but he felt no pain.

They rounded the far turn and came down the homestretch. Alec saw Henry standing in the middle of the track waving his hat. It was funny to think that Henry believed he could stop them by waving his hat! They swept past him and under the finish wire, both horses continuing to race around the track until their strides began to falter and their heads began to droop.

The rhythm of their hoofs became uneven, then picked up again only to become irregular once more.

At long last, their run was reduced to a gallop, then to a lope and finally to a trot. They came to a stop at the far end of the backstretch, breathing hard, their sides heaving and trembling, and with their heads hung low. They had run themselves into the ground, as Alec had feared. Both were beaten.

News and Sympathy

12

The reporter was the first to speak. "We have just shared a spectacular adventure," he said.

The other men remained silent. Stunned, they watched the two horses on the far side of the track. Then their gazes shifted to Henry, who was picking himself up from the middle of the track where he had fallen.

"In all my years I never saw anything like it," one onlooker said solemnly.

"I'm not even capable of saying what I saw," another said. "I even forgot to stop my watch. That ain't never happened to me before."

"You're not alone," a third said. "None of us caught the fractions."

"You're some clockers," the reporter said half-jokingly, half-seriously. "You're so overwhelmed by two working horses you forget to push the stems of your watches."

"You just don't see horses work like that," one man said. "It was the way they went at each other!"

The reporter made a penciled note, then asked, "Do you think this . . . ah, island invader . . . that's a good name, I think I'll use it . . . worked exceptionally well, or was the Black below his best form this morning?"

One of the clockers said, "He was in his best form, all right. Alec couldn't hold him."

"You can't blame Alec," another explained. "When the Black wants to run like that, nobody can hold him."

"Tell Henry that and he won't believe you. The old man's worried to death."

"I don't blame him. He's got the Black's bad foot to worry about."

The reporter made another note. "A champion and a *potential* champion went at it hammer and tongs this morning," he read aloud. He paused to ask the man next to him, "Cliff; does that sound all right to you? I mean, referring to Flame as a potential champion? I'd like to say that knowledgeable horsemen like yourself are now inclined to take Flame very seriously."

"No horse could have stayed with the Black the way he did without having quality and class," Cliff answered solemnly.

The reporter turned back to his notebook. "Then Flame is no freak," he said. "He is no product of Hialeah's press agentry but the genuine article, having proved it this morning by storming alongside the Black with an irresistible drive that had the champion reeling."

"You'd better make it that both horses were reeling," Cliff corrected.

"Flame's headlong style of running," the reporter went on, "may change the complexion of the Hialeah Turf Cup this coming Saturday. The swashbuckling island invader is destined—"

Another clocker interrupted. "Bill," he said, "you'd better just hold onto your story awhile. From the looks of those two horses neither may be running in the Cup race. They both checked and bobbled toward the last."

"They look all right now," the reporter said, watching the two horses on their way back. "Sure, they're blowing, but what do you expect after a workout like that?"

"If you can't tell by the way they're moving, take a look at Henry's face. You can read it there."

The reporter turned to Henry who was still standing motionless in the middle of the track, his face ashen-white.

"He looks pretty mad," the reporter said.

"Not mad. Sad," came the clocker's reply. "If the Black is sore going back to the barn, Henry will keep him out of the Turf Cup."

"Nothing is certain until both horses cool out," another said.

"The Black looks sound enough to me," the reporter said.

"He looks better than I expected," another said. "I could have sworn they'd both broken down. They sprawled near the end."

The Black and Flame neared the gap in the fence. They walked slowly but, it appeared, soundly. There was no fury in their eyes, only an overwhelming tiredness. Their ribs rose and fell with their rapid breathing, their eyes were red-rimmed, and lather

covered their coats. No longer were their strides those
of lofty, imperial monarchs. Only quiet dignity remained beneath the sweat and dirt. Perhaps the
invisible fires still burned. None who watched could
be sure.

The two stallions staggered as they approached the
tunnel beneath the stands, and rocked on the springs
of their legs, one tired foot following another. The
interplay of muscle was there for all to see but so was
the immense fatigue. Every movement appeared
torturous. The cool morning breeze played with their
manes and tails and this, perhaps to some extent,
soothed them.

"They'll be all right," one man said.

"Maybe," another answered. "I hope so. I sure do.
A few hours from now and we'll know."

It was noon when Alec left the Black and walked to
the most distant of the barns where Flame was
stabled. The area was quiet except for an occasional
message to a trainer through the loudspeaker system.
Alec found he jumped every time it crackled. There
was no doubt his nerves were on edge. A few
late-working horses were being cooled out and walked
monotonously around the plots of grass in front of
their barns. He found that he was studying each of
their steps to see if they walked soundly, a conse-
quence of the past few hours he'd spent with the Black
and Henry.

The Black had stopped blowing soon after being
washed down; his wind had presented them with no

problem. It was only after a full hour of walking that Henry had said, "Well, we might as well get him ready to go home."

"You're kidding!" Alec had exclaimed.

"No, not at all. His foot is bothering him again, and I'm not going to take any chances racing him."

"Get Doc Palmer. You can't be sure otherwise."

"I've already sent for him," Henry had answered. He was not angry with Alec for what had happened, nor at himself or Flame or Steve Duncan. He was just very tired.

The veterinarian had arrived and the x-ray pictures had been taken. They showed no broken bones, but the slight swelling indicated the old injury had been aggravated. It was probably nothing serious, Dr. Palmer had said. He'd know more within three days' time. Meanwhile, the Black should be kept as quiet as possible.

The press and photographers had been there, and Henry had told them that the Black would not run in the Hialeah Turf Cup. "We can't take a chance," he had said. "There's too much ahead of us to risk a race that soon. We'll see what the Doc says next week before making any further plans."

Alec knew that the evening newspaper headlines would read something like BAD FOOT PUTS CHAMPION ON SHELF, and that thousands of racing fans would be disappointed.

Now that he was through work for the morning, Alec wanted to see Steve Duncan. He continued through the barn area, stopping occasionally to talk to grooms and trainers. He tried to conceal his anxiety but failed miserably.

"I hear you had some tough luck, Alec," a trainer said.

"Not too bad. He'll be all right." But Alec never had been any good at whistling in the dark. His track friends could read him like a book.

"Sure, he's fine, just fine. He'll be back soon," Alec said repeatedly. "A little trouble, that's all."

He stopped at one barn to talk to a red-haired groom who visited the Black most every day. "Don," he said, "you look awful. What's the matter?"

"Nothin' but a bad night to get over," the man said lightly. But his voice, like his eyes, were sympathetic and understanding.

"It's just a slight hoof injury," Alec said. "There's really nothing to worry about. A few days and he'll be as good as ever. Doc Palmer said so."

"Sure, Doc would know, if anybody would. But it's the same foot, isn't it? It could be lots longer."

"Yeah." The unbearable tension hung over them. "Well, I got to go now," Alec said.

"I heard that other horse cooled out okay," Don said.

"That's good. I was hoping he would."

"That's racing," the other returned dismally.

Alec took another path around the barns, knowing he'd meet fewer friends along that route. It wasn't easy trying to put up a front when everybody knew the Black's injury could be serious enough to put him out of racing altogether. As the veterinarian had said, they'd know for sure in three days' time. Until then all he could do was hope for the best and try to look less concerned than he actually was. He had a tough horse. If they had to go home, he would try to be as tough as the Black and go without bitterness toward Steve Duncan.

The stable area on the far side was deserted. It was as Alec had wanted it, and he sat down to think.

Should he help Steve Duncan or not? If so, he would have to get over his anger toward Steve for prompting the kind of a workout that never should have taken place. It was intentional on Steve's part, of course. He had wanted to impress those who were watching, and he had done that only too well. He would have gotten his permit to race at half the speed Flame had worked.

But, Alec told himself, Steve had not been able to control Flame any more than he himself had been able to manage the Black. Once the pace had increased to its fevered pitch, they had been riders, nothing more. They had witnessed, more than participated in, the workout. It had not been racing but an uncontrolled, dangerous battle. If others had not been aware of it, he was.

Also, Alec reminded himself, he had agreed to letting the two horses work together, even urging Henry to allow it. He had wanted to help Steve Duncan. Did he still want to, now that the Black was sidelined? Could he possibly forget his bitterness and give Steve some advice that might help him when he raced? Flame had all the speed in the world, but he would not have a clear track on race day as he'd had this morning. There were things Steve had to learn.

There was a small group of men, including a photographer, standing outside Flame's stall when Alec arrived.

"Hey, Alec," a sports columnist called, "the rumor's going around that the Black really broke down. That's tragic, real tragic."

"Just a rumor," Alec said. "It's nothing serious." He studied the man, who didn't seem to be too unhappy over another fellow's misfortune. Some reporters were like that. They thought that bad news made good copy. It sold more newspapers.

"That's a terrible thing to happen so late in the day," the columnist went on, "after his being trained and aimed for the Turf Cup race, that is."

"He's not the first horse to be scratched from a race," Alec said, a little annoyed. "We'll point him for another race now."

"Is he lame?"

"No. Henry just doesn't want to risk any chance of further injury by racing on Saturday."

The columnist prodded. "It wouldn't be that he doesn't want to risk being beaten by an outsider, would it?"

Alec didn't answer. He brushed by the man and went over to Steve. "Can I see you alone for a few minutes?" he asked.

"Sure, Alec. But I don't want to leave Flame just yet."

There was a screen over the top half of the stall door and Alec could make out Flame's small head behind it. Steve's friend Phil Pitcher was standing guard, still wearing his sun hat and knee-length shorts and still looking very worried.

"This horse is a ham, Alec," the photographer said. "You should have seen him. He posed every time I held up the camera."

"If he was a little less tired, he would've kicked it out of your hand," the sports columnist commented. Then, turning to Steve Duncan, he said, "I got a few more questions. I'm not so good I can interview horses, and you haven't given me much copy yet."

"I've told you just about everything that happened," Steve said uncomfortably. It was obvious that he was unused to handling newsmen. He didn't like being the official host.

"Do you think your horse can beat the Black in a race?" the columnist asked.

"It's a matter of luck," Steve answered, looking at Alec.

"Come on, now. You can do better than that."

"We won't be racing the Black anyway."

"Not in the Turf Cup race," the columnist admitted. "But if you do any good in that race you'll go in the Widener Handicap the following week, won't you? The Black should be in it, too, if he's not broken down altogether."

"One race was all we figured on," Steve said uneasily.

"You mean you'd pass up the hundred-thousand-dollar Widener if you had a chance to get some of the money?"

"I hadn't given it any thought," Steve said.

The columnist smiled. "That's better. One race at a time. Is that the way you want me to put it in my column?"

"Something like that," Steve replied defensively.

"Good. I'll make it that upon interviewing Steve Duncan after his electrifying workout on Flame this morning, I found him to be a real veteran despite his riding apprenticeship. He was calm, collected and convinced that Flame deserved a chance in both the Hialeah Turf Cup and the Widener Handicap."

Steve said nothing.

"Your horse cooled out completely sound, didn't he?" the columnist asked Steve.

"Yes, he did."

"Can you account for his standing up so well after such a workout?"

"He had the foundation under him. He's run hundreds of miles. He's dead fit."

"Hundreds of miles," the columnist repeated puzzledly. "But where? Where's he done all this running?"

Only then, Alec noted, did Steve Duncan exert any of the self-confidence that had been apparent in his first visit to Hialeah.

"That's all I've got to say," he said, ending the interview.

A little later when they were alone Alec told Steve, "You handled your press 'conference' pretty well for the first time."

Steve said, "I'm still too fuzzy-chinned for the likes of that columnist."

"He'd make it tough even if you had a beard down to your belt. You did okay."

"I'll do better next time."

Alec studied Steve's serious face. There was no doubt he was confident there would be a next time, as winner of the Turf Cup race. "Yes," Alec said finally. "I guess you will at that."

Their eyes met and Steve said, "You're sore, aren't you?"

"Wouldn't you be with a lame horse?" asked Alec. "We ran our horses into the ground."

"Flame got away from me."

"You said you could control him. He took my horse with him, so I had no control either."

"The Black did something to him that I never felt before. It was the next thing to fear, I think."

"It was rough on both of them," Alec conceded. "Whatever accounted for it isn't important now. It's done."

"I'm sorry. If there was anything I could do . . ."

"There isn't."

For a moment they were silent, then Steve spoke. "Like I said, I'm sorry about the Black, but with him out of the race next week we'll win, Alec. I'm not afraid of any other horse."

"Then you'd better start," Alec said quietly. "A horse like yours can get into plenty of trouble. Every horse in the race next week will be as formidable as Flame and his superior in experience and rating. That goes for their riders, too. You won't be dealing with a bunch of inexperienced kids."

"Like me?" Steve asked.

"Like you," Alec said evenly.

"Flame can make his own holes in any field," Steve said.

"I doubt it. You'll go down fast if he tries it. He'll need guidance, and that will be up to you."

"And you don't think I can do it?"

"Not on the basis of what I saw this morning. You've got a chance only if you can put Flame where you want him on the track. You won't know what tactics to use until you see how the race is going. Only then can you decide on strategy."

"I can stay in front and keep clear of any trouble," Steve suggested, his face a mirror of sincerity.

"Not if horses break from the gate in front of you . . . and they will. There are a couple with lots of early speed, front runners both of them."

"Then I'll lay in the pack, and come on when I find racing room."

"There may not be any."

"Then, like I said before, Flame will make his own holes."

"And as I said before, he'll go down, taking you with him," Alec answered. "You don't win these races on speed and guts alone, no matter how much your horse may have."

"You mean I've got to be lucky, too," Steve said, smiling. "You once told me that luck has more to do with success on the track than anything else."

"I don't remember going that far, but luck *is* a big factor in any race."

"Okay, Alec," Steve said, serious again. "I know you're trying to help me. How do I win the race doing it *your* way?"

"It's not *my* way," Alec said, "and there's no sure thing in racing. But it's important that you know not only what to expect from Flame but from every horse in the race . . . all of them and their riders. There are certain things we know from past performance, and that's what I'm here to tell you. First, let's take Gustavo Carballido who will be up on Bolero . . ."

The stable area was quiet except for Alec's voice as he went on, calmly and steadily, acquainting Steve Duncan with the horses and riders he'd be racing in the Hialeah Turf Cup. It was fully an hour later before they parted and went their separate ways, each going back to his own horse and dreaming his own dreams.

Turf Splendor

13

It was a sunny, hot and humid afternoon for the running of the Hialeah Turf Cup. The red-coated bugler, wearing shiny black boots and a black hunting cap, stood in the middle of the track. He placed a long coach horn to his lips, the sun glistening on the golden instrument. The music came forth, sounding the call to the post.

On the roof of the grandstand, television cameras were ready to pick up the horses as they emerged from the paddock tunnel onto the track. The television sportscaster told the nation's viewers, "We're at Hialeah Park in Florida where some of the world's top racehorses are about to come on the track for the running of the Hialeah Turf Cup. It is the nation's oldest grass stakes race and is contested at a distance of a mile and a half for a gross value of about one hundred thousand dollars. A unique feature of the Hialeah Turf Cup is its international aspect, for a preponderance of foreign-bred horses have competed in the race during the past decade, and, we might add, have won it. All in all the Turf Cup has been quite a profitable affair for horses from across the seas, and this year may prove no exception. Horses from

Argentina, Chile, Ireland and the United Kingdom will be competing against American-bred campaigners over the grass course.

"The field of fifteen turf specialists is a surprisingly large one—or, at least, larger than was expected—due to the withdrawal of the Black from the race, following a recurrence of a hoof injury suffered during a workout a few days ago. The U.S. champion would have been the 'strong' horse in this race and many of the horses going to the post today would not have started if he had run as scheduled.

"And now," the sportscaster continued, "the horses are coming onto the track."

The sleek horses, some accompanied by stable ponies, emerged from the paddock tunnel, their jockeys standing in stirrup irons. They skittered through the crush of people lining the corridor, their coats and riders' silks glittering in the bright sun. The first horse danced onto the track to begin the post parade.

"That's Bolero on your screen now," the sportscaster said. "He hasn't fared too well at Hialeah but should fancy today's long route of a mile and a half, especially with the flashy Gustavo Carballido guiding him. They're both from the Argentine, Bolero being owned by Mario Garcia-Pena of Buenos Aires.

"The number two horse is another Latin invader, El Mono from Chile, being ridden by one of the United States' most successful riders, Jay Pratt. The public has made this pair the favorite. El Mono has great capability on the grass and is in top form. It is not surprising that his Chilean owner, Louis Citron, gave this riding assignment to Jay Pratt, for Pratt is no stranger to foreign horses. He has raced all over the world and probably has more mileage to his credit than an astronaut.

"Number three is Windswept, the United States' main threat to beat the foreign invaders over the long distance of the Turf Cup. He has the reliable Pete Edge aboard. The public has made Windswept second choice, knowing he is more partial to grass than dirt and is razor-sharp at this time.

"Number four is Erin Sea from Ireland, making his first start in the United States. He is being ridden by the veteran jockey Nick Marchione.

"Number five is another U.S. threat, Tartan, and he will be guided by young Willy Walsh. Tartan won an impressive race over the dirt track last week in his Hialeah debut and last fall performed brilliantly on the grass in New York. This will be his first grass invasion of the year."

Flame was the next horse to be introduced in the post parade. For a few seconds the sportscaster was silent, watching, along with his viewers and those at the track, the antics of the horse as he refused to stay in line. Breaking from his rider's hands, he swept past the stands and a spontaneous wave of applause from the crowd followed him as he went along; the television cameras stayed on him.

"The number six horse," the sportscaster said finally, "is the surprise entry, Flame, winner of the Nassau Cup in record-breaking time a few weeks ago. He is being ridden by the apprentice Steve Duncan, who seems to be having a difficult time controlling him as you can see. Flame is receiving quite an ovation from the crowd, a remarkable thing for a horse making his debut. His coat is a glistening chestnut color and he stands well over sixteen hands. His presence has brought back to the race some of the glamour it lost when the Black had to be withdrawn. The two horses competed in an explosive workout a few mornings ago which no doubt accounts for the applause now being given Flame. While he will have to prove his mettle in the race, he is adding additional luster to a most colorful post parade."

The camera shifted to the next horse in line. "Number seven is High Ruler from England . . ."

In the crowded stands Henry Dailey watched Flame gallop down the turf stretch of the infield course. He told Alec, sitting beside him, "That horse's action is as beautiful as anything I've ever seen. He'll be able to handle grass as well as he did dirt the other morning."

"He's smooth, all right," Alec admitted. Watching Flame in action from a seat in the grandstand was far different from racing alongside him.

Applause for Flame broke out in the stands around them, and Henry said, "Your friend Steve ought to be pleased to get a hand like that. It tops many an ovation I've heard *after* a race has been won."

"It won't matter much to Steve," Alec answered. "All he cares about is the seventy-thousand-dollar winner's purse hanging on the wire. He aims to get it."

"So do fourteen other riders," Henry returned. "Your friend's not the only one who thinks money is more important than applause." He leaned back in his seat. "Hooking up with riders like these is a tough way to make a buck."

"I told him what to watch for," Alec said.

"Pete Edge on Windswept is almost certain to set a sizzling pace," Henry commented.

"I told Steve not to go with him."

"If he does, he'll have a dead horse under him coming into the stretch run."

"But sometimes Pete tries to fool you," Alec said. "He'll set a false pace that only looks fast, then he doesn't fall back but keeps going on to win."

"I know. I've seen him get away with it many times. And Pete's only one of the experienced riders your friend Steve will have to contend with. You're expecting too much of him, Alec."

"I'm expecting nothing."

"He won't even know what kind of a pace is being set," Henry went on. "You can't take a kid off the streets and in a few hours teach him what's taken others years to learn."

"I told him all that," Alec said defensively. "I just told him what to look for out there. Some of it he'll remember. Most of it he won't."

Henry turned his attention back to the horses as they went behind the starting gate. "With a big field like this," he said, "a race is just as much a test of jockeys as it is of horses. The rider with the most skill could win without having the best horse."

Flame suddenly reared, almost unseating Steve Duncan.

"He plays rough," Henry said. "He might just fly to

pieces in the gate. He might go right out of gear and not race at all."

"He's keyed up, but so are the others," Alec said.

"He's dripping more water from his flanks than any of them."

"It could be the weather," Alec said. "It's hot and muggy."

"You're trying to sell yourself on that horse, Alec. What's he to you, anyway? He wouldn't be the first horse with morning speed that's failed miserably when put with horses of established class in the afternoon. A race is the only way to find out what sort of a horse Flame really is."

"I was thinking more of Steve," Alec said quietly. "It takes a lot of courage to ride in this kind of a race without any experience at all."

"Courage or recklessness," Henry grunted. "Take your pick."

Alec didn't answer. His eyes were on the starting gate as the metal doors closed. He recalled how it had been for him the first time, and he knew how Steve felt. The huge crowd was still, awaiting the break. The fronds of the tall palm trees hung motionless in the air. The doors suddenly swung open, the bell clanged, the red flag dropped and the Hialeah Turf Cup had begun!

Flame stumbled as he was leaving the gate but quickly recovered. Steve steadied his horse before moving on again. It seemed to him that some of the horses were leaving the gate at ninety miles an hour, breaking so quickly they looked as if they had gotten away from their riders. Flame was floundering and bouncing up and down, but Steve wasn't worried over the fact that the others were outrunning him from the gate. The long distance was all in his favor. He would hug the inner hedge all the way and make up ground when he could, knifing his way through the field at every opportunity.

The field swept by the stands for the first time, the early speed specialists far in front and Flame being edged over against the inner hedge by a horse racing alongside and brushing against him. Steve still wasn't worried. It was a long run to the first turn and, somehow, he would get Flame clear. The horse alongside swerved against them again, and Steve gave more ground for fear of going down.

Flame was running into stinging dirt and clods of earth being kicked into his face by the pack in front of him. It was something he'd never felt before. He stopped abruptly, then aimed for the inner hedge to get free of the flying dirt. Steve didn't yank him away. He let go of his head and let him see what he was running into, hoping he'd have enough sense to change his mind. The ground was whizzing by. Within seconds Steve knew that if Flame tried to burst through the hedge he'd have to decide whether to stay in the saddle or bail out.

Flame decided things for him. He turned away from the hedge and swerved into the horse running alongside. He rammed his way through and burst into the middle of the pack with Steve trying to guide him.

Up ahead the lead was changing often, first one and then another horse having control of the race even before they had run the first quarter of a mile. A plucky small horse met the challenge of the hulking brute beside him and went into the lead, only to have another horse come up on the outside and race beside him as they approached the turn.

Steve recalled that Alec had told him a killing pace might well bring about the downfall of many of the horses, that he should be content to sit back and wait. He would have liked to rate Flame as Alec had suggested. It would have been nice to place Flame anywhere on the track he chose . . . but Flame wasn't that kind of a horse.

Another racer moved alongside, keeping Flame pinned and trapped behind the wall of horses in front of him. Steve turned Flame over toward the hedge. He'd be in a pocket there, too, but at least he'd be saving ground going around the turn. From there he'd watch his rivals' moves, conserving Flame's speed for later. His horse was being rated after all—necessarily so, for there was no place for him to go. For a while, he was hopelessly out of the race.

On the far outside of the racing pack, Steve saw a horse charging down on the leaders from the number 14 post position. He was angling across the track, trying to pass the field before it reached the turn. Running hard, he just made it and stole the lead from the small gray horse. Then, suddenly, he slowed up, almost causing a disastrous spill behind him as jockeys brought their mounts almost to a standstill to avoid racing into him.

Things got tight for Steve, too. He took hold of Flame and, standing almost upright in his stirrups, backed up against a horse behind him. The jockey yelled, and Steve knew he couldn't hold Flame there any longer. He swung Flame away from the hedge, trying at the same time to avoid running up on the heels of the horse in front of him. He did all he could to stop Flame but his horse was full of run. Flame bolted and tripped against the horse in front. He almost went down, but recovered, missing the flashing hoofs only by inches.

Steve knew he couldn't stay where he was a second longer. He took a tighter grip on the reins, yelled at the other jockeys and moved out! He cleared the heels of another horse, but one racing on the outside blocked his way. Once more he took strong hold of Flame.

As the field swept around the first turn there was no chance for Steve to find racing room and get in the clear. He was now as frustrated as his horse. And he knew that the other riders were making it tough for him. He told himself that the long backstretch was made to order for Flame, that all he had to do was wait. For a while he had no place to go. He had to be patient, as Alec had said. He had to learn from his mistakes, and he'd made quite a few already.

Starting down the backstretch the pace continued incredibly fast and the lead was fiercely contested. Steve saw the lead change five times ahead of him, with only about six lengths separating all fifteen horses in the race. He and Flame were still trapped in the middle of the pack and, it seemed, would never have a chance to move out.

He saw a horse whiz through along the rail and move up quickly to take the lead. Then the small gray horse racing on the outside lowered his head and dug in again, regaining the lead. He was a trim little horse, his strides as balanced as his body. The pace he was setting might kill off most of the others, and Steve wished he could remember whether he was part of the Argentine entry that Alec had said were the horses to watch. One would go out in front and keep the others busy, while his entry mate would hang back in the pack and come on later to finish the job in the homestretch. Steve glanced at the horses racing beside him, wondering if the gray's stable mate could be one of these. They were closing the gap gradually on the flying leaders, forcing the little horse to dig in more and more.

Flame had his ears pricked up, Steve noticed, and seemed to be taking things more easily than before. Perhaps they were both learning to bide their time. He must keep him in stride; that was most important. Steve decided he would have to make the right decision when the next chance came to move up. There was a big jam in front again. He must wait. He mustn't move prematurely.

Now! A horse bore out in the middle of the backstretch and Steve moved Flame inside and up a length. Another horse gave up the ghost and Steve went around him, moving one length closer to the front of the pack. Slowly, he was taking Flame through the field like a football runner going through a line. Steve felt his confidence mounting; he gave Flame another notch in the reins.

He improved his position still more. He found the openings he was looking for, swinging around two horses racing abreast and knifing inside a third who was tiring and bearing out. Approaching the final turn, he came flying out of the pack directly behind the trailblazers!

The horse in third position was beginning to tire and his rider was having a bad time with him. He wanted to bear out, going wide around the turn. He took Flame with him and Steve knew he had no alternative but to go around the tiring horse and lose ground doing it. It was part of racing luck.

The tiring horse brushed against Flame, and racing quarters got tight, but Steve held his position and burst ahead when the tiring horse labored still more. Once clear, Steve moved Flame over to the hedge again, bending with him as they swept around the turn. Just ahead, the little gray horse was faltering and giving up the lead to a hard-running bay who, Steve decided, must be his stable mate. The two horses and riders were exchanging places like two members of a relay team.

Steve gave Flame another notch in the reins and concentrated on the two leaders as he came off the turn and entered the homestretch. The gray horse began bearing out at the top of the stretch and his rider tried to hold him in line. The horse was responding to his jockey's urging even though no whip was being used; what achieved this result was the man's hands and his remarkable coordination with his mount.

Now, Steve knew, the chips were down, and the final test was at hand. He saw the hole on the inside, left for him by the jockey in front. He knew better than to go in there and be trapped again, which is what the rider on the small horse probably wanted. His mount was dying fast under him but he might be able to hold him together if Steve took Flame into the pocket.

Steve steadied Flame, trying to decide whether to go around the tiring horse or wait for him to fall back. He had a fresh horse under him. To save time, if not ground, he would take a chance and challenge from the outside.

When he made his move, his rival excitedly used his whip, surging forward dramatically. Steve was unprepared for the burst in speed, having thought he'd have no trouble disposing of the rapidly tiring horse in his challenge to the leader. The small gray began bearing out under the pressure of his rider's whip, taking Flame to the middle of the track with him.

Steve saw the jockey switch his whip from one hand to the other in an effort to straighten out his horse. He made the change with the dexterity of a baton twirler and the swiftness of a magician, never losing control of his reins or his horse. He hit hard and often, his strokes matching his mount's strides in rhythm. The gray was frightened into giving extra effort but the horse continued to bear out, blocking Flame.

Steve saw the big bay leader racing in isolated splendor along the hedge, only an eighth of a mile away from the finish line! Quickly, he decided to change course again and go inside. As he was about to check Flame, the small horse in front of him buckled and quit, leaving the track clear!

Taking advantage of the first break he'd had in the

race, Steve gave Flame his head. Luck was with him now just as it had been against him earlier. Flame moved past the gray horse as if jet-propelled. The tunnel of noise which was the homestretch erupted in new frenzy as Flame was turned loose. It was as if he had been dawdling throughout the race and only now was running! He slammed through the stretch in his drive for victory. He carried the fight to a grimly struggling leader whose rider was using his whip strenuously, as if knowing from the noise of the crowd that a disaster was about to overtake him. Flame's ears were pinned back against his head as he raced all-out, closing with a rush that would not be denied. He passed the leader and went on, opening up daylight between them, and thus ending the Hialeah Turf Cup.

Flame and Steve had proved their mettle.

The Big Two

14

That night the newspapers and television sportscasters were comparing Flame to the Black. The "Big One" had now become the "Big Two" at Hialeah Park. Flame's splendor and brilliance in his triumph had convinced everybody that no horse but the Black could stay with him. There were those who believed, too, that Flame the challenger could turn back the champion as easily as he had the distinguished field in the Hialeah Turf Cup.

The sports commentators and writers beat their news drums in anticipation of the race between the Big Two. It was hoped that the Black would recover from his foot injury and be sound enough to race in the Widener Handicap the following Saturday. Flame, having won the Turf Cup, was automatically made eligible for the Widener. It would be Hialeah's outstanding race of the year. It would attract people from all over the world, this race between the United States champion and an outstanding challenger from the United Kingdom.

No longer was Flame referred to as an outsider, an islander, or a phantom horse. All the questions about his racing ability that had been obscure before the

Hialeah Turf Cup had been answered. Now he towered over all the foreign horses racing at Hialeah. He was a worthy challenger from the United Kingdom. Some sports commentators went so far as to say that if the Black was not in his very best form, the Widener Handicap was sure to go to the invader.

Only one sportscaster, Count Cornwell, after referring to the Turf Cup race as Flame's "lawn party," cast some doubt on the challenger's effectiveness against the Black. "It remains to be seen," he told his audience that night, "what the challenger can do on the dirt. Just because a horse can run a winning race on the grass doesn't mean that he can win on the main track. Those who are hailing Flame as the new champion after his smashing, record-shattering race today are a little premature. There's a chance the dirt may be to Flame's disadvantage, especially if the going happens to be heavy. It is well to remember that the Black has proved his ability to carry weight over a distance and still win time after time, under all manner of track conditions. . . ."

The next morning Alec wanted to find out if Steve intended to race Flame in the Widener Handicap. He'd won all the money he needed to buy his island. Yet, races worth over $100,000 were tempting to anyone who had a chance of getting some of the prize money. Flame had demonstrated very impressively that the Widener Cup, filled to the brim with dollars, was within Steve's grasp. Only the Black might keep him from taking it home.

When Alec reached the distant barns he found that

this day too belonged to Flame. A party was going on and Flame was the guest of honor. He had his handsome head over his stall's half-door and tubs of goodies were placed in white pails in front of it. There were carrots, celery and lettuce—none of which he was eating—all arranged for the photographers who were taking pictures. Hialeah's press agentry was there, directing the photographers, and Steve was standing beside his horse.

Alec remained in the background, watching Steve. The boy seemed relaxed, even agreeable, and eager to talk about Flame's triumph to the newsmen. It was only natural that Steve should be happy over the festivities, Alec mused. The tense hours of last week were a thing of the past for him. He and his horse had made good in a most impressive way.

Alec remained at the far end of the row, waiting for the photographers to leave. He sat on a tack trunk and watched some blanketed horses being cooled out after their morning workouts. A small radio blared in his ear but he didn't bother to move away from it.

A groom walked his charge close by. "Alec," he said, "you going with the Black on Saturday?"

"It looks like we might, but Henry wants to wait a few more days before making up his mind."

"No sense rushing the old warrior," the groom said.

"You mean the Black or Henry?" Alec asked, smiling.

The groom spewed a stream of tobacco juice and said, "I mean Henry. Guys his age never make up their minds until the last minute anyway. No matter what. You can't rush 'em, ever."

"He's just being cautious," Alec said. "But Doc Palmer told him that the Black's foot is okay again."

"Overcautious about everything, that's Henry," the groom went on sagely. "I worked for lots of guys his age. The Black's fit, all right. I seen you slow-galloping him this morning. He didn't miss a beat."

Alec nodded. "But Henry's the boss," he said.

"One-hundred-thousand-dollar races don't come up every weekend," the groom said. "You might remind Henry of that." He looked up the row to where the party for Flame was breaking up. "I wouldn't worry none about that horse, either. He's just added a little spice to the handicap division. Let them have their fun, Alec. You and the Black will take 'em over next Saturday."

A few minutes later Alec moved up the row. Steve was sitting alone on the tack trunk, his booted feet up on a chair, his face thoughtful.

"Quite a party you had," Alec said.

Steve nodded and pulled up his legs so that Alec could sit down. "Some kind of promotion thing," he said.

"It looked like fun."

"It was, I guess . . . in a way."

"Sometimes things like that help relieve track boredom," Alec said. "It's good for horses as well as people."

"I'm not bored," Steve said.

"No reason you should be after yesterday."

"They made a lot of fuss about it, all right."

"But not about nothing," Alec said. "It's the hunting cry of the herd. You made good. What's it going to be next, Steve? The Widener? Or are you going home?"

Steve pushed his back against the wall. "I'm not making up my mind today," he said. "I'm going to wait."

"You're as bad as Henry," Alec said, jokingly. "If neither the Black nor Flame race in the Widener, the press department can promote the 'Big Nothing'."

Steve didn't return Alec's smile. "You think I should go home like I said, don't you?"

"That's strictly up to you to decide," Alec answered. "All I know is that you got the money you needed in one fell swoop, which is surprising, to say the least."

"But I could use still more," Steve said.

"I know what you mean," Alec said quietly. "When anyone's got a chance to pick up a piece of a race worth over a hundred thousand dollars, he'll go for it. It's only natural."

"I didn't say I was going to race. I haven't decided yet."

"You will," Alec said, certain of what he saw in Steve's eyes. "But don't hurt your horse. He might not be able to handle dirt the way he did grass."

"He can handle *anything*," Steve said. "*Any* kind of track. *Any* kind of horse."

"I wouldn't be too sure."

Steve shrugged his shoulders. "If we don't get first money, we'll get second money. That should be over twenty-five thousand," he said, becoming cautious and agreeable.

"Then there's about thirteen thousand dollars for third place and sixty-five hundred for fourth," Alec added.

Steve smiled. "Four good reasons for my going in the Widener."

"But the big reason is the first money," Alec said. "Something around ninety thousand dollars."

"It would be nice," Steve admitted. "It's there for the asking, especially if the Black doesn't start."

Alec shrugged his shoulders. "Perhaps, but every race is different, Steve. You made a lot of mistakes yesterday. You were lucky to get a clear path at all. You might not be so lucky the next time out."

"Maybe I learned more than you think I did," Steve said.

"Maybe you did. I hope so."

"I won't get caught inside next time."

"You made other mistakes, too," Alec said.

Steve's face clouded a bit. "Flame ran his race. We won. What more do you want?"

"You cut in too sharply on the first turn."

"I know, but somebody bumped me."

"You were too close. You almost went down."

"They clipped our heels."

"You should have taken more hold."

"Flame only runs faster when I take hold."

"You've got to do more than hang on."

Steve shrugged his shoulders and stood up. "I know you mean well, Alec, but you never rode a horse like Flame."

"I know the kind of horse you're talking about," Alec said quietly. "But let's leave it your way." He turned and walked away. "I'll see you around," he added.

Alec knew that the Widener Handicap would be

between the Big Two, just as the press and the public wanted. Steve had definitely made up his mind to go after more of the big money. And it was only a question of a day or so before Henry decided that no island horse was going to challenge the Black's supremacy and get away with it . . . not without a fight, anyway.

Butterflies

15

Monday morning came the track handicapper's long-awaited announcement of the weights for Saturday's $100,000 Widener Handicap, and immediately afterward the press was interviewing Henry Dailey.

"You ought to feel pretty good, Henry," one reporter said. "The Black was assigned only a hundred and thirty-six pounds."

"Only?" Henry asked. "That's top weight for the race, isn't it? Has any other Widener horse ever carried more?"

"No, of course not. But the Black's not like any other Widener horse. Actually, a hundred thirty-six pounds is no more than he carried in his first race here, and he won that in a cakewalk. We expected him to pick up a few more pounds off that race, anyway." He paused before asking, "There's no doubt you'll go with him now, is there?"

"We'll go with him if he stays sound this week," Henry answered. "The weight assignment suits us fine."

The reporters glanced at their mimeographed sheets listing the track handicapper's weights for the Widener. "How do you figure Flame's package being

only six pounds lighter than the Black's?" one queried.
"He's been given a hundred and thirty pounds."

"He won Saturday, didn't he?" Henry asked. "And impressively. So he impressed the handicapper with his speed, too. It seems like a pretty good job of handicapping to me."

"With only a hundred thirty-six pounds on the Black you ought to feel that way," the reporter said.

"There you go using *only* again," Henry said with a grin. He didn't intend to try to hide his pleasure over the weight assignments.

Another reporter said, "At these weights there aren't going to be many starters Saturday." He glanced at his mimeographed sheet. Fifty-three nominees were listed, with weight assignments ranging from the Black's top weight of 136 pounds down to the lightest-burdened horse of 108 pounds. "Trainers who had planned to run their horses will be scared off. I doubt more than four or five will be brave enough to go to the post with the Black at a hundred and thirty-six."

Henry shrugged his shoulders. "That's their problem," he said. "They're getting up to twenty-eight pounds difference, scaling down to a hundred and eight. Some of them should try to surprise us."

"Some of them will, I suppose," the reporter said.

"Weight can stop a train," Henry said. "You know that as well as I do."

"One hundred and thirty-six pounds won't stop the Black. I know that, too," the reporter answered.

"What are you guys driving at?" Henry asked. "You think our horse should be carrying more?"

"Or Flame less," the reporter said cagily.

"He won at a mile and a half, didn't he?" Henry asked.

"It was his first start and it was on grass," the reporter reminded Henry. "I think he should have gotten in the Widener at lighter weight since the Black's impost wasn't raised off his last race."

Henry turned away. "Leave the handicapping to the handicapper," he said. "You stick to news writing." Ignoring the reporters, he watched a stable dog lapping coffee from a saucer in Alec's hand. "If you think Flame's getting a bad deal, see the handicapper about it," he added. "Or go see Steve Duncan and get his views on the subject. You got mine. I'm not sayin' any more."

After leaving Henry Dailey, the reporters approached Steve Duncan and the boy told them, "Sure, a hundred and thirty pounds is more than I expected, but we're going to take a shot at it anyway. I still think we've got a good chance of beating the Black."

Then they went to the track handicapper for a public statement regarding his weight assignments for the Widener Handicap. He said brusquely, "I don't need to give any explanation."

"It's only that if we're surprised by your weights, the public will be, too," a reporter announced diplomatically. "We expected the Black to carry more than a hundred and thirty-six pounds."

"I can't see penalizing a good horse out of competition," the handicapper said. "At a hundred and thirty-six pounds he's carrying more than any other horse in the history of the Widener. If I put more weight on him, he might break down—"

"Or Henry Dailey might decide not to race him," one newsman interjected.

"That's true, too," the handicapper admitted grudgingly. "The Black's an exceptional horse but there's a limit to what he should be asked to carry."

"Besides," another reporter commented, "the people want to see him run, and you don't want to do anything to keep him from starting. Is that it?"

"Yes, and as far as the rest of the Widener nominees are concerned, I won't put a premium on mediocrity. If they're in with a champion, they've got to expect to race with at least a hundred and eight pounds on their backs."

"You gave most of the field less weight than usual, but you went up on Flame. I guess that's what surprises us most. How come?"

"He ran a sensational race last Saturday," the handicapper replied. "Any horse that can shatter the turf record at a mile and a half should be able to carry a hundred and thirty pounds over a mile and a quarter."

"But this one's on the dirt."

"I watched him closely. His action convinced me he can handle dirt as well as grass."

"If he does, the Black's in for a race," the reporter said.

"So is the public," the handicapper said. "With just six pounds difference between the Big Two, they should come down to the wire together."

"The Big Two," the reporter repeated. "Is your job track publicity or handicapping horses?"

"In this case, both," the handicapper answered quietly.

Race tension continued to mount during the rest of the week. Alec didn't go near Steve Duncan's barn and Henry scheduled their workouts so that the Black was never on the track the same time as Flame.

The Black worked easily for Alec, and gave no indication that he was favoring his injured foot. Sharp and eager to go, he was tremendously impressive as he sizzled around the track. He drew rave notices from all the professional horsemen and early-morning devotees who watched him. Never had he run better or looked better, they agreed. He well deserved everything said of him during his illustrious career.

The Black completed his week's work by making the fastest run of his training period, and a sports columnist wrote, "The Black is the People's Horse and, I believe, will prove himself worthy of their confidence this coming Saturday in the Widener. To tangle with him is to be turned loose with a tiger. Only Alec Ramsay could handle him, and he does a masterly job of it. Alec rides with the poise and dignity of a true championship rider. He remains cool and self-possessed at all times, which is especially essential in this business of race riding. Surely he belongs with the great jockeys of all time.

"The Black is running fire these days and he stirs admiration, fear or respect, depending upon whose corner you're in. Those who are looking for the challenger Flame to dethrone him were frightened to death this morning when the Black finished a brilliant work. There is no doubt the coming Widener will be a dramatic race. Already the drama is unfolding. It has color and tradition. It has a champion and a worthy challenger. It has captured the interest and imagination of racing fans throughout the world. Saturday is the day!"

The following afternoon between races Flame appeared on the track for a public workout, his last before the big race. He went a mile and an eighth carrying 130 pounds, the same burden he'd tote on Saturday. He had the crowd gasping at his speed. He was clocked in the sensational time of 1:50 on a muddy, holding track without being urged by his rider.

That evening Count Cornwell told his television audience, "Saturday's Widener will not be just another purse-proud winter race. That was made even more apparent this afternoon by Flame's public workout under the 130-pound package he must carry in the Widener. This horse can make a watch run backward, and despite the Black's star quality there were many in the stands today who thought Flame could and would beat him on Saturday. Each year, tracks throughout the country post fortunes in the high hope of arranging such spontaneous 'box office' as the Widener will have on Saturday. More often than not it doesn't materialize. But this Saturday the Widener has it. This will be a really big race. One is well aware of it as the day approaches."

Hialeah's public relations department did its best, too, to assure the public that the coming Widener would be a smashing horse race between the champi-

on, the Black, and the challenger, Flame. A large
supply of buttons were made available early in the
week reading "I like the Black" and "I like Flame."
They were distributed to the weekday crowds and
everybody was wearing one or the other. Everybody
was taking sides. No one asked about the other horses
who might be going to the post. It was a foregone
conclusion that the Widener Handicap would be a
smasher of a race between the Big Two. It was the talk
of Miami, and Hialeah Park looked forward to one of
its largest crowds in history.

The press box itself added more fuel to the fire by
taking a poll among the nation's newspaper represen-
tatives. The results were twelve votes for the Black
and twelve votes for Flame.

"Those two horses are just as close together in
speed as the vote was," a New York City newsman
said. "I have to stick to the Black until he's beaten, but
I know, too, that the Widener is going to be a real epic
in the annals of racing."

"I voted for Flame," another from Chicago said.
"This is the magic city of Miami and as the magic hour
approaches, I look for some fast sleight-of-hand work
on the part of Steve Duncan. Duncan is a hot
apprentice rider and it looks to me as if he'll continue
to sizzle along with his horse, barring the unforeseen.
He has a natural talent for race riding despite his lack
of experience. He has a way with this horse and he
uses his head to get the most out of him. Flame is not a
normal racing machine. He defies explanation. He
runs like the wind and yet Duncan is able to guide
him. He's getting in the Widener six pounds lighter

than the Black. That difference in weight, although slight, could mean victory for Flame."

The track publicity director read all the news stories and told a colleague, "The plot thickens, just like in the pulps. We've got the biggest race we ever had on our hands."

On Friday, as almost everyone had expected, the names of only six horses of fifty-three nominees were dropped in the entry box for the Widener Handicap. In addition to the Black and Flame, the lightly weighted Mad Wizard at 108 pounds was entered, along with Apache and Sail Away at 110 pounds, and Bronze Prince at 112 pounds.

"It's not that we're so brave," the trainer of Apache told the press. "We're just hungry for that third and fourth place money. None of us have much hope of getting more than that."

"It's never safe to underplay the lightweights," one reporter commented. "Apache has a world of natural speed to go to the front, and a big concession of twenty-seven pounds to maybe stay there."

"Both the Black and Flame run their best races from off the pace," Apache's trainer answered. "They could give us twenty pounds more and still come on to beat us. Like I said, we're racing for third and fourth place money, nothing more. You won't get me to say we got our hopes aimed at anything higher."

The newsmen proceeded through the stable area, wondering how Henry Dailey was standing up under pre-race pressure. They found him watering petunia beds in front of the barn while Alec sat nearby.

"How do I feel about tomorrow?" Henry repeated, when asked. "I guess I feel pretty good."

"Then Flame doesn't worry you too much?"

"I leave most of my worrying to the younger fellows," Henry answered. "If the Black isn't ready to run his race tomorrow, it's too late to do much about it now."

The newsmen turned to Alec. "And you, Alec? You got any stomach butterflies?"

"Sure," Alec said. "I got 'em, always just before a big race. As Henry says, he leaves the stomach jump-ups to us younger fellows."

They turned back to Henry, and one said, "You're used to saddling horses for big folding money. Isn't that right, Henry? That's why you get no butterflies."

"Guess so," Henry said, still watering his petunias.

"You'll have no excuses if Flame beats you, then," the reporter persisted. "The Black is all set to go."

"No excuses at all," Henry admitted. "He's pretty tight, and a race last week would have helped him a lot. But he's ready to go tomorrow; that's all I can ask of him."

"The race looks like a tossup to a lot of people."

"That's what horse racing is all about," Henry said. He looked up from his petunias. "What kind of last-minute comment did you get from Steve Duncan? Did he tell you his horse was going to whip us tomorrow?"

"No, he didn't."

"What did he say then?"

"He said, 'No comment'."

"That's the smartest talk I've heard all day," Henry said, smiling. "He's learning fast."

"No, we think he was just pretty sick to his stomach," a reporter answered. "He was green in the face."

"Oh," Henry said, turning back to his petunias.

It was early evening when Alec and Henry walked around the empty track, their feet sinking deep in the sandy loam. It was part of their regular pre-race routine. Alec stayed near the rail, his eyes on the track furrows. He knew the surface would be all cut up again the next morning by working horses; then it would be harrowed and manicured before the races in the afternoon. However, there was no way in the world he could have gotten out of this walk, needless though it might be. Psychologically, it did something for Henry—and perhaps for himself, too.

"There's a hole, Alec," the old man said. "Stomp on it good."

Alec pushed dirt into the hole with his foot, stomping the ground flat until Henry was satisfied.

"I don't want you to get caught on the rail tomorrow," the trainer said. "Stay a good length off it. It's too soft."

"Yes, Henry."

"There's another hole. I'll get it."

"Okay."

"This is very important," the trainer said. "It can mean the difference between your winning and losing."

"I know, Henry." Alec watched the trainer fill in

the hole. He knew that after walking around the track, they'd return to the barn and Henry would draw a picture. *The oval is one and one-eighth miles*, he'd put down on paper. *Distance from judges' stand to first turn, 325 feet. Distance from last turn to finish, 1,075 feet. Width of track, 80 feet.* And so on, until it was all there to be gone over again and again. That was the way Henry did things the night before a race, and somehow it helped relieve their tension. It was better than sitting around doing nothing, Alec conceded.

"How are you feelin'?" Henry asked.

"Fine," Alec said.

"You've got good judgment of pace," Henry said. "Make sure you use it tomorrow. Don't let any of those lightweights steal the race from you, Apache especially. With all his speed he just might go the full distance, carrying a hundred and ten pounds."

"I'll remember," Alec said.

"Anyone can be guilty of making a mistake in judgment," Henry went on.

"I'll try not to," Alec promised.

"If you do make any mistakes, try to make the right ones."

"I won't mess it up," Alec said.

"Watch your friend Steve every second," Henry cautioned. "He's got a natural talent for riding and he's good with that horse of his. One would never believe he didn't know what the inside of the winner's circle looked like a week ago."

"He's come a long way," Alec admitted.

Henry filled another hole in the track and said,

"He's had a good teacher since he got here."

Alec shrugged his shoulders. "I only did for him what I've done for others starting out."

Henry looked at Alec. "I know, but this time it might backfire on you. Steve's got a good idea what to do in a race now. Make sure he don't beat you by a nose."

"I'll do my best," Alec said.

"I want you to do more than your best," Henry said solemnly. "You might have to . . . *to win.*"

Later that night Henry got an early morning edition of a Saturday newspaper in the hope of reading himself to sleep. Instead, it kept him awake most of the night.

"BIG TWO" CLASH IN WIDENER TODAY
Unbeaten Flame Challenges Champion

Hialeah, Fla. Feb. 21—Undefeated Flame will attempt to reduce the "Big Two" to the "Big One" this afternoon when he opposes the Black, handicap champion, and four others in the Widener Handicap at one mile and a quarter.

This running of the winter classic shapes up as the finest in its long history. The Black, in defense of his championship laurels, will carry 136 pounds, while Flame will get in with 130. It is this difference of six pounds which many experts feel will give the challenger an edge in the run to the finish wire. The possibility of the Black being beaten has attracted nationwide, even worldwide interest to this year's

$100,000 Widener. Never in the Black's long career in attaining turfdom's highest laurels will he be so hard-pressed to retain his supremacy over the handicap ranks. . . ."

Henry feared Flame more than he had let Alec or anyone else know. The greatest horse and rider could be guilty of making mistakes during the running of a grueling race, and tomorrow it would take just one false move by the Black or Alec for the Widener to be lost to them. He wished he could quiet the butterflies in his stomach.

Scale Up, Scale Down

16

An hour before the running of the Widener Handicap, Alec warmed up the Black under the tall Australian pines which lined the sandy road through the stable area. When he had finished, he knew his horse was supple and alert for the job ahead of him.

Henry held the Black's bridle while Alec slid down from the stallion's back. "I want you to gallop him in front of the stands, too," the old trainer said. "Break him out of the post parade the first chance you get. Gallop him all the way into the backstretch before turning him and going back to the gate. I want him warmed up and in his best stride when the gate opens, not after racing two or three furlongs like maybe some of the others."

"I know, Henry," Alec answered. The trainer's instructions were nothing new to him. He'd heard them every race day. But if it helped Henry to repeat them each time, he would listen.

"Get into your working clothes now," Henry added. "We'll see you in the paddock."

The jockeys' room was noisy and crowded. Alec went to his locker and sat down on the bench. Those who were riding in the big race appeared calm, but

Alec knew that inwardly they felt as he did, pretty uneasy if not filled with anxiety. It couldn't be otherwise with so much money hanging on the finish wire; the winning rider would get ten percent of the purse, about $9,000 for just two minutes of racing time. It was enough to put anyone's nerves on edge.

Willy Walsh munched a grilled cheese sandwich and talked casually to a reporter about the chances of Mad Wizard winning the race. "He's out of his class," the young jockey said frankly, "but we might be up there somewhere, light-weighted like he is. He's an honest horse. He tries all the way."

Nearby, Jay Pratt had shucked off his custom-tailored street suit and was pulling on his skin-tight white nylon pants. He looked out the window, watching the big crowd in the paddock. The bigger the crowd, the better he liked it and, usually, the better he rode.

Turning back to his locker, Pratt caught Alec watching him. "It's a juicy bundle of boodle we'll be racing for today," he said quietly.

"It's that, all right," Alec returned, pulling on his pants.

Pete Edge was already dressed in his silks and playing Ping-Pong with a rider who didn't have a mount in the Widener. He smashed the ball hard, as if trying to get rid of a lot of excess steam.

The veteran Nick Marchione was in his silks, too, and playing cards at the far end of the room.

Reaching into his locker, Alec took out his black-and-white checkered blouse and pulled it over his T-shirt. Tucking it in his pants, he moved closer to where Steve Duncan, fully dressed in red silks, was sitting on a trunk. Steve had a couple of sportswriters around him, but he didn't seem to be annoyed. He chatted with them as he might have done with any other visitors.

Alec decided that Steve had come a long way in his give and take with the press. There was no fear or timidity in his face. Instead, it showed a kind of exaltation. He had straddled all the horsepower a rider could put under himself, and at this point in his short career he was a hero, a jockey to be interviewed and a rider with whom to reckon.

The roar of the crowd watching the finish of the race preceding the Widener Handicap filled the room. Alec turned away from Steve Duncan.

An old friend, the sports editor of a New York daily newspaper, came up to him. "Hi, Leo," Alec said. "I was wondering why I hadn't seen you around this winter."

"I left New York only this morning," the man said. "It was five below."

"Then be glad you're here," Alec said, buttoning his blouse.

"I am, but I'd like to be able to stay the rest of the winter."

"Why don't you? You've been at it long enough to pick your spots."

"They need me in the office."

The man turned, nodding his head toward Steve Duncan. "What about that kid and his horse? Are they everything I've read?"

"For publication?" Alec sat down on the bench, pulling on his boots.

"No, just for me."

"One robin doesn't make a spring," Alec said quietly.

"But it gives a man hope of seeing another robin," the newspaperman returned. "That was a pretty big race he went to last week."

"I didn't say it wasn't."

"I know what you said. One big race doesn't make a horse or rider. Still . . ."

Alec finished pulling on his boots and reached into his locker for his goggles. "You asked me what I thought, and I told you. I'm not saying I'm right. I only believe it was too big a race for Steve Duncan. He needs as much guidance as his horse does. Last week's race came too soon for him and too fast. He has a lot more to learn about racing before—"

Turning around, Alec stopped suddenly, for Steve Duncan was standing there, his face a fiery red. Alec said nothing, and it was Steve who broke the strained silence. "You keep out of my way, Alec," he said angrily. "Just keep out of my way."

When he had gone, the newspaperman said, "I see what you mean. He's hot."

"He's no iceman, that's for sure," Alec said. "I guess he thinks now that I'm jealous of his success."

"Or, worse still, that you're contemptuous of his riding," the man added. "It's the way a lot of young riders feel at the beginning. He'll learn fast."

"But not fast enough for this race," Alec said,

picking up his helmet and goggles. "It's time to weigh-out. I'll be seeing you, Leo."

"Lots of luck, Alec."

"Thanks, Leo."

The clerk of the scales had an easy job ahead of him, weighing out the jockeys for the Widener Handicap. There had been many entries for most of the other races on the afternoon program; it had been something of a task to get all the riders on the scales and out of the room in time for their races. He glanced at the six riders who now stood in line, waiting patiently to be checked out. Beside them were their valets, supplied by the track, to assist with the tack.

Willy Walsh, bareheaded and wearing blue-and-yellow silks, stepped on the official scale first. The needle swung to 100 pounds and steadied. His valet handed him a three-pound saddle and a pad containing five pounds of lead. The scale needle went up to 108 pounds. Willy was the lightest weighted of the field.

"Okay," the clerk said. "Walsh. Number one. At one hundred and eight pounds. Check." Watching the little rider hand back his tack to the valet, he added, "You're getting skinnier every day, Willy. You'd better watch yourself or you'll just waste away."

Willy Walsh picked up the number 1 armband from the rack and slipped it over his right arm. "How else am I goin' to ride these lightweights?" he asked, grinning and shrugging his narrow shoulders.

The clerk liked Willy Walsh, as he did most of the riders in the room. They were men of integrity, men who worked hard at their trade, men with whom he was proud to be associated. Only occasionally did he watch any of them race. He was always too busy in the big room. It didn't matter. He wasn't interested in racing so much as he was in the men themselves. He knew them and their ways well. He had only to watch them play Ping-Pong or cards or just sit around, day after day, to know how they rode a race.

Willy might be skinny but he was game right down to the last ounce. He always strutted around the room like a fighting cock, not actually looking for a fight but not avoiding one either. He kept himself in top physical condition.

Jay Pratt was the next rider to step on the scale. He was as slick and polished as always and looked very handsome in his orange-and-green silks. The valet handed him his tack and the needle settled at 110 pounds. Riding Apache at that light weight made Pratt one to watch, the clerk decided. It might even be the combination he'd back himself, if he were out there in the stands.

"Pratt. Number two. At one hundred and ten pounds. Check," he said, watching the unsmiling rider step off the scale.

Always deadly serious, that was Jay Pratt, the clerk decided. Nothing ever showed in his face. He was a man who could sit by himself in a corner of the room and stay apart from almost anything that went on. He never disclosed impatience, never got ruffled or annoyed at anything that went wrong. That was the way he rode, too, sitting back and waiting until the other riders thought he had done his best. Then he'd come on with a rush, still calm and cool but slamming home.

"Okay. Next," the clerk said, and baldheaded Nick Marchione stepped on the scale. "You'll never make it, Nick," he said, grinning broadly.

The valet handed Nick Marchione his saddle and pad of lead; the needle stopped at 110 pounds. The veteran jockey smiled toothlessly. "When I can't make one hundred and ten, I'll quit," he said.

"That'll be the day," the clerk answered, watching the rider clad in silks of baby pink step down from the scale. The colors made him look ridiculous, but Nick didn't seem to mind. Only the horse they represented mattered, and if Nick didn't think Sail Away had a chance in the big race, he wouldn't be riding.

"Marchione. Number three," the clerk said. "At one hundred and ten pounds. Check."

He watched the veteran jockey slip the number 3 band on his arm, and wished Nick would quit riding. They were the same age, fifty-one, and had known each other for many years. More often than not, he felt twice Nick's age. What did it was seeing his friend go to the post day after day when he himself found it hard to do anything more strenuous than walking. Nick raced as hard as ever and had won more races than any other rider in the country. He still got up bright and early in the morning and worked horses. He had all the money he'd ever need but financial security didn't seem as important to him as winning races.

Still watching the veteran jockey, the clerk shrugged his shoulders. There wasn't any reason for Nick to quit, he admitted to himself. Nick was proud of his profession and he showed it the best way he knew how—by riding. He had good hands, strength and an uncanny sense of pace. He wouldn't quit until he was carried off the track. The clerk hoped it wouldn't be today.

Pete Edge hopped on the scale in full regalia, complete with saddle and the belt containing strips of lead which he had taken from his valet. The needle went to 112 pounds.

"I'm always surprised when you make this weight," the clerk said, studying Pete's blocklike figure which seemed better suited to boxing than to riding.

"I spent the night in the steam box," Edge said. "I got a good horse. I had to make it."·

The clerk nodded. Yes, Pete Edge on Bronze Prince at only 112 pounds was another combination to watch. Maybe the Big Two wouldn't have the race to themselves as most people thought. He watched the rider step down in his silver-gray silks and said, "Edge. Number four. At one hundred and twelve pounds. Check."

As Pete Edge moved away, the clerk watched him. Pete might get beaten but he too would never quit. He had more drive, energy and determination than any other rider in the room. He was from the old school whose motto was "Fight and survive or be knocked down and remain behind." Win or lose, he'd make every other rider know they'd been in a horse race. His hands seemed to be made of steel, and some of the boys said that Pete could keep a tiring horse going by brute strength alone.

Pete's only trouble in the jockeys' room, if one could call it trouble, was that he was honest and candid to a fault. He always said what he thought and would stand up to anyone twice his size, if necessary. So a big horse like the Black wouldn't faze him a bit.

Alec Ramsay stepped on the scale in his black-and-white silks. The valet handed him a worn old saddle which the clerk knew had been used by Henry Dailey during his riding days. Across the saddle was placed a pad, the pockets of which were filled with heavy strips of lead.

As the needle climbed to 136 pounds Alec said, "I'll never get used to carrying this much lead, Bob."

"Don't you mind," the clerk said, "just as long as your horse doesn't object to it."

"He'd better not," Alec said, smiling.

"Not today," the clerk agreed. "Okay, Alec, hop off. Ramsay," he called. "Number five. At one hundred and thirty-six pounds. Check."

He watched Alec go to the number rack. Here was another rider who made racing worthwhile for him. Alec was potentially one of the great riders of all time, but the clerk doubted he'd be around the jockeys' room very long. Instead, Alec would become a successful trainer. He wasn't interested just in his own horse but in *all* horses. He seemed to have studied every horse at Hialeah and knew more about them than any other rider at the track. Most of the other jocks were too busy concentrating on their own mounts to bother about anyone else's. And yet this knowledge of horseflesh must have helped Alec become the successful rider he was. When the other riders wanted to know anything about a field, they asked Alec. He always told them, too, never keeping anything to himself. That was another reason he was so well liked—that, and his having saved the hides of a good many jocks as he'd done for Willy Walsh a few weeks ago.

The boys said Alec rode a race with the precision and balance of a well-oiled machine. The clerk thought there was more to it than that. Alec was no machine; instead, he seemed to be part of his horse when he was riding.

Steve Duncan, wearing crimson silks, was the last to step on the scale. When the valet handed him his saddle and pad of lead, the needle went up to 130 pounds.

The clerk smiled at the apprentice rider. "I'm sure you're not used to picking up so much lead, young fellow," he said.

Duncan didn't return the clerk's smile. He seemed angry and very intent, but the clerk attributed it to pre-race anxiety. That would disappear the moment Duncan mounted his horse.

"Duncan. Number six. At one hundred and thirty pounds. Check," the clerk concluded. He hoped this kid would be all right in the big one. He'd have his hands full riding against the others. It took more than a sensational mount to win the Widener. If Duncan wasn't careful he might lose not only the race but a limb as well. It was that kind of a race. It couldn't be otherwise with a purse of $90,000 hanging on the wire.

The official weighing-out for the Widener Handicap had been completed. The riders put on their protective helmets and left the room.

"Lots of luck, fellows," the clerk called. "Hurry back now."

The Widener Handicap

17

The searching cameras of the television network were mounted high on a platform outside the paddock. They caught the field of six horses leaving their saddling stalls and walking around the ring, their bodies, glistening in the sun, as colorful as their riders' silks.

The television sportscaster spoke to his vast nation-wide audience. "The Widener Handicap has drawn a record-breaking attendance of over forty-five thousand fans to Hialeah Park on this sunny but cool day in February," he said. "Six top handicap performers are poised for the big race over the classic distance of a mile and a quarter. Heading the field is the Black, United States champion, who is carrying the silks of Hopeful Farm and is top weighted at one hundred thirty-six pounds. There he is now on your screens, being ridden by Alec Ramsay, who is known to have one of the best heads of any jockey now active. That's Henry Dailey, his trainer, walking alongside."

Suddenly the Black bolted, scattering the crowd on the paddock rail.

The telecaster said, "The Black looks like a champion and acts like one. Seeing him in the full bloom of his career is a new and exciting experience for a great number of people here at Hialeah today. It is estimated that at least an extra ten thousand patrons have turned out because of his presence."

The cameras continued to follow the Black around the ring as the telecaster went on. "A close second choice of the large crowd here today is Flame, an island horse, representing the United Kingdom. He captivated the public last Saturday by winning the Hialeah Turf Cup in record-shattering time, and there are many who believe this foreign challenger can match strides with the Black. It is the anticipation of such a duel between the Big Two, as they are being called, that has brought international attention to this year's Widener."

Flame had come to an abrupt stop and was looking at the crowd outside the paddock ring, his ears pricked up.

The sportscaster commented, "A noted trainer told me a short while ago that Flame is the most inquisitive horse he's ever seen at a track. And as you can see on your screens, Flame is very nervous. The white lather about his loins is known as 'washing' and horsemen are not inclined to enjoy seeing it on their horses just prior to a race. However, Flame was 'washy' last week before a large paddock crowd and went on to score a considerable upset. Today he will be attempting to pull an even bigger trick, that of beating the mighty Black.

"He is being ridden by the apprentice jockey Steve Duncan and will carry one hundred and thirty pounds, six less than the champion."

The cameras switched to the other horses as the call to the post sounded. The sportscaster continued, "The lightweights in the field are not being overlooked by the crowd. There are many fans who believe these horses will be strong contenders in the race, despite the presence of the Big Two. Number one is Mad Wizard with the young and very popular Willy Walsh up. He is toting the featherweight of only one hundred and eight pounds, and has a high turn of speed that makes him dangerous in any company. He can carry his lick a mile and a quarter, too, providing there isn't a lot of pressure put on him in the early stages of the race.

"The number two horse is Apache with the very successful Jay Pratt in the saddle, making a total package of one hundred and ten pounds. Pratt has won more races at Hialeah this season than any other rider. Apache has the reputation of being a 'sometime' horse, turning in a good race one day and a bad one the next time out. His trainer told us earlier that he believes Apache is ready for a top effort. If so, Apache with Jay Pratt in the saddle will be a combination to watch.

"Number three is Sail Away with the veteran Nick Marchione up for another one hundred and ten pounds. Sail Away is one of the most determined and consistent horses in racing today, seldom racing out of the money. He is a very workmanlike animal, going about the business at hand soberly and most effectively. During four years of hard racing at all the major tracks in the country, Sail Away has given his best every time he's gone to the post. With the greatest rider in the country to guide him today, Sail Away should be a strong contender in the homestretch.

"And here's another fighting horse who wants to win every time out. Number four is Bronze Prince with Pete Edge up for a total of one hundred and twelve pounds. Racing fans know that Bronze Prince is a money horse. He runs best from off the pace, and usually has to overcome the disadvantage of a nonchalant start. Often during the running of a race he has been disregarded until the stretch run, and then comes boiling down on the leaders in the last few strides to get the money. Today he has a rider whose courage equals his own. Bronze Prince and Pete Edge might well provide a distinct surprise at the finish of this race."

The horses disappeared within the tunnel, but the cameras on the grandstand roof picked them up again as they emerged from the other side and stepped onto the track. As the post parade began, the sportscaster continued, "Today's Widener could be one of the great contests of all time in America. Races like this don't come along very often. It takes more than rich purses at popular major tracks to achieve them. It takes more than the genius of press agentry or the showmanship of Broadway. It takes luck . . . and luck this year for the Widener came not only in the presence of the Black, United States champion, but in the form of Flame, an unknown island horse who came to Hialeah Park via Nassau. Despite the great records of all the horses racing for the Widener Cup, it is Flame who is filling the principal role in this drama to prevent the Black from extending his dominion to international dimensions. We will know in a matter of minutes if Flame, the foreign challenger, can live up to his star billing."

Alec moved the Black into the number 5 starting stall, satisfied that his horse had been warmed up just as Henry had wanted. He had taken him all the way into the backstretch before returning to the gate in front of the stands. It should not take the Black long to get into his best stride. He was supple enough, alert enough to move to the attack the moment the gate was sprung.

Flame was putting on a show for the crowded stands, rearing skyward as an assistant starter sought to grab his bridle and lead him into the gate. But despite his antics, he seemed to be under control. Steve had good hold of him and with no further trouble Flame walked into his starting stall. The boy's face radiated confidence, perhaps, like his horse, responding to the fans' applause.

Alec turned away. He thought of Steve Duncan only as a competitor now and no longer a friend in need of help and advice. Steve was on his own.

The Black banged against the sides of his stall and Alec spoke to him softly, telling him to wait, that soon they'd be off and running. He knew his horse would be able to handle the top weight of 136 pounds, and their next-to-outside post position was better than being closer to the rail. Even with all the warm-up, the Black might be late in breaking from the gate. At least, though, there was no chance of their being pinned on the rail today.

He saw Willy Walsh in the number 1 stall, all set to go. Light-weighted as Mad Wizard was, Willy wouldn't have any trouble getting him out of there. Mad Wizard had the early speed to go to the front immediately, but Alec didn't think Willy would keep him in the lead very long. He'd be afraid Mad Wizard might get lonesome out there all by himself and start looking around for company. Willy would take hold once they were free of the pack, saving his horse's speed for later on. But Alec knew he couldn't be sure of anything today.

Only when the race was under way would he know what Willy's tactics would be. There was no telling what any of the riders would do, regardless of past performances, until the moment of decision came. They were all good enough to contrive a masterpiece of riding from beginning to the end. He could win on the fastest horse only if he made no mistakes.

Alec steadied the Black and looked through the grilled door in front of him. He learned something new in every race he rode. This kind of knowledge, of a practical nature, was the only kind in which he had any confidence. He hadn't been able to learn it from Henry or anyone else. Within a few seconds, he would have a lot of decisions to make. He had to have enough confidence in himself to make them quickly. If he hesitated, he'd lose the race. He had to avoid jams. He had to sense what was going to happen *before* it happened.

Flame bumped against the sides of the adjacent stall, but Alec didn't turn his way. He ignored all the horses in the gate, just as he did the clamoring crowd.

All that mattered was the track in front of him. There
was a slight haze overhead and a breeze came up from
the south, blowing stronger and stronger in his face.
He sat quietly astride his horse. The Black had lost his
skittishness and was quiet, too. So was the crowd.
Everybody awaited the start of the race.

The gate doors flew open and the bell clanged. Alec
shouted at the top of his voice, as did all the other
riders. The Widener Handicap was on!

The Black broke easily as the horses plunged ahead.
Alec watched the riders as well as their mounts.
Apache had outbroken the field but Jay Pratt wanted
no part of the lead; he was already holding back to
prove it. Willy Walsh sent the feather-footed Mad
Wizard to the front, bolting away from the tangled
stampede behind him. Jay Pratt kept backing off
Apache from the early pace and was fourth as the
racing field passed the stands for the first time.

Alec restrained the Black, keeping him in fifth
position, where he could see what the other riders
would do. Right from the start the masterminding of
the jockeys had begun. Willy Walsh wasn't taking hold
of Mad Wizard but letting him go on. Jay Pratt was
backing off Apache still more. Nick Marchione had
Sail Away just off the pace in second position, putting
pressure on Mad Wizard. Pete Edge was scraping the
rail, trying to squeeze Bronze Prince on the inside of
Sail Away. He was taking a big chance for Nick wasn't
giving him much racing room. But Pete Edge would-
n't quit trying. He drove his horse through an opening
and alongside Sail Away. The run to the first turn was
shaping up as a veritable duel between the two riders

while Willy Walsh on Mad Wizard was a stride ahead of them.

Alec watched Jay Pratt and all the other riders up front. He kept sizing them up, almost in the manner of a boxer studying his opponents. Only Steve Duncan was missing; he was in back somewhere. The Black was striding easily as they approached the first turn. Alec was surprised to find himself within hailing distance of the leaders, for he knew Willy Walsh was setting a sizzling pace for the first quarter of a mile. The Black kept moving ahead and Alec leaned into the turn with him.

They were off Apache's hindquarters and just outside of him when Jay Pratt let his horse drift out a bit. For a few seconds Alec was uneasy, waiting for some indication that Apache was going to change his path. The two horses were at a "heel clipping" stage. If he'd been a little farther back he could have dropped to the inside of Apache. As it was, in order to go inside now he would have to slow down the Black or gamble that he still had enough room to take him in *over* Apache's heels. He decided quickly that it wasn't worth the gamble at this early stage of the race. Both horses might go down if they clipped heels.

He made his decision to stay on the outside of Apache going around the turn. Once they had completed the turn and were in the backstretch he would make his move to the front.

A few seconds later, Alec realized that Apache wasn't continuing his route around the turn but was floating out still more to the center of the track! Alec waited for Pratt to straighten up his mount, but

Apache continued to move out, taking the Black with him! Alec began checking the Black, not wanting to lose any more ground to the front runners. He'd made a bad decision, but there was still time to correct it.

As he took the Black back, almost choking his horse in order to get him on the inside of Apache, Flame suddenly appeared from out of nowhere. He swept by along the inner rail, closing the gap between himself and the leaders. Steve Duncan was in the race!

Alec tucked the Black in behind Flame. Steve was trying to split the flying pair directly ahead of him, but Nick Marchione and Pete Edge wouldn't let him through. Alec saw Steve settle back in his saddle, content to wait. The Black was flying now, but so were the others. The pace was going to be very swift going down the backstretch.

As the horses moved into the backstretch it was, as Alec had thought it would be, a rider's battle all the way. Willy Walsh called upon Mad Wizard for still more speed as Nick Marchione and Pete Edge kept pressure on him. Flame was full of run in fourth place, despite the blazing pace. Again, Steve tried to get through between the two flying horses in front of him. Failing, he took Flame back a stride and then loomed strongly on the outside of Sail Away and Bronze Prince.

The Black moved closer to the pack but Alec kept good hold of him and stayed near the rail. It was no time to make a move with the spine-tingling battle going on ahead of him. He would save the Black's speed and stamina until the jam broke in front. It was still anybody's race.

Willy Walsh had Mad Wizard still in front, holding on to his slim lead despite the awesome pressure that was being maintained behind him by Pete Edge and Nick Marchione. Willy seemed determined to stay in front, an ambitious project with a horse that was known to go a distance only if allowed to set his own leisurely pace.

Pete Edge had Bronze Prince right on top of Mad Wizard and was fighting for every foot of ground around the race track. Nick Marchione was just outside them and had gone for his whip. The swashbuckling, powerful Sail Away responded to Nick's urging and moved more to the center of the track, blocking Flame when he attempted to pass again. Once more, Steve had to drop back to avoid Sail Away's heels but came on again stoutly from the inside.

Nearing the final turn, Mad Wizard began tiring and Willy Walsh went for his whip. Mad Wizard drifted a little wide and Pete Edge took advantage of the rail opening, sending Bronze Prince to the inside of the flying leader.

But Willy Walsh was not going to give way. He brought his mount on again, moving once more into the lead. It was Willy's fling at greatness.

Alec gave the Black another notch in the reins and his horse took advantage of it, ready and anxious to begin his powerful drive to the finish. Alec had to make up his mind quickly whether or not to make a move on the turn or wait for the stretch run. A lot depended upon what happened up forward. He didn't want to have to check the Black as he'd done on the first turn. This close to home it might cost him the race. He'd have to make the right decision fast. He watched the other riders closely. Somewhere behind him was Jay Pratt who would be coming on any second with Apache. Jay had an uncanny sense of pace and was not a rider to be considered "dead" before the homestretch.

The horses roared into the final bend with a rush. The last quarter mile of the Widener Handicap was coming up and the tension, both on the track and in the stands, mounted. Already it had been as exciting a horse race as was ever run, and once more a big shuffle was developing!

Mad Wizard, on the rail, was holding his lead over Bronze Prince by a head. Sail Away was another head behind and on the outside. Flame was coming on again, trying to get by all of them. The Black was starting to move, and coming up from behind was Apache. This race was not just between the Big Two. It could be called the race of the Big Six!

There was a deafening roar as Pete Edge went for his whip for the first time. *Whack*, he blasted Bronze Prince in an effort to move ahead of Mad Wizard. *Whack, whack, whack*, he blasted him again. But it didn't do any good. Pete Edge put away his whip, and Mad Wizard retained his lead by a head going around the turn.

Alec decided quickly not to make his move until he was in the homestretch, for things were popping ahead. When Pete Edge stopped using his whip on Bronze Prince, Nick Marchione went for his. The veteran rider gave Sail Away two hard smacks on the left side in order to get him clear of Bronze Prince's heels. As a result, he was right in Flame's path again! Alec saw Steve check his mount quickly and almost go down!

Nick Marchione was switching his whip from his left to his right hand when it flew out of his grasp. That didn't stop him. He smacked Sail Away barehanded and the courageous horse responded, inching up on the outside of Mad Wizard. The three leaders pounded around the turn with Flame regaining stride and going after them.

Alec gave the Black more rein and moved up behind Flame, where he'd be able to challenge at the top of the homestretch.

The crowd was on its feet as the horses came off the turn. Once again, Pete Edge went for his whip, trying to get Bronze Prince ahead of Mad Wizard in a desperate lunge. He whipped and slashed at his mount's hide but Bronze Prince was through. The horse faded quickly despite all Pete Edge could do.

Alec saw the opening left by Bronze Prince on the rail and guided the Black toward it. Instinctively he'd made his decision for the run down the homestretch. He was going on the *inside* of the front runners rather than around them in his drive for the finish. There would be no time for a second choice or for regrets; the wire was less than a quarter of a mile away. The racing field had now entered the corridor of noise, and pandemónium reigned. Alec sent the Black into an all-out drive. Their final move had begun!

Far on the outside and coming off the turn was Apache, with Jay Pratt rocking in the saddle. They, too, were going all-out during the last stage of the Widener!

Willy Walsh saw the Black forging his way through along the rail, trying to pass on the *inside* of his horse. For a second he thought of whacking Mad Wizard again. It was a temptation to use his whip at this crucial moment but his cool head advised against it. Mad Wizard was giving this race everything he had and it wouldn't do any good to hit him. Willy stashed his whip; it would be a hand ride all the way to the finish, regardless of the outcome. With the reins alone he spoke to his horse, his lips unmoving. "Come on, horse," he said. "Hold yourself together a little longer. You're not as tired as you think you are. You've got me to hold you up. Don't let this big black bull get by you."

Willy felt Mad Wizard flatten out still more and move closer to the rail. There was barely room for the Black to get through, and Willy hoped Alec wouldn't insist upon trying it. He didn't like to think of Alec going down.

Mad Wizard dug in, his head still in front of the tightly packed group. Willy Walsh fairly lifted his tired mount and hurled him forward! The huge crowd gasped, for it seemed at that moment that the young rider and his horse were going to bring about one of the most spectacular upsets in racing! After setting a record-shattering pace, Willy was coaxing and cajoling Mad Wizard to go the full mile and a quarter and win! It was a peerless riding performance, perhaps equaled in the annals of racing but never excelled. The cheers of the crowd rose to new heights as Mad

Wizard lengthened his lead to a half-length with less than an eighth of a mile to go!

Alec knew that the opening between the rail and Mad Wizard was almost too narrow for him to squeeze into but he couldn't hesitate any longer. He took the Black *over* Mad Wizard's heels and felt his own leg burn against the rail. *Close but not down.* Now they were inside where nobody could get them out! The Black made up the length on Mad Wizard in one stride.

Willy Walsh glanced over his left shoulder when the Black came alongside, hard against the rail. "Go get it, Alec!" he yelled, but he didn't give another inch of racing room or stop hurling his own mount forward.

On the outside of Mad Wizard, Nick Marchione berated himself for losing his whip but kept hitting Sail Away with his bare hand in the fight for the wire. He felt his mount strain every time he slapped him hard. It was as if Sail Away were going to break himself in half in order to get ahead. He had run a long race, a hard race. . . . Suddenly, Nick felt his horse break from beneath him and he knew they were through. Sail Away swerved, bumping into Flame who was coming up alongside. The red horse missed a stride but Steve Duncan steadied him and they went on. Nick Marchione regretted he wasn't going to be in on the finish. It was going to be a corker!

Alec passed Willy Walsh, their two mounts running shoulder to shoulder. The Black was still dangerously close to going down and Mad Wizard, whipped to a frazzle, continued to display rare courage under Willy's urging. Alec saw Flame move out on the other side of Mad Wizard. On the far outside of the track Apache was driving for the wire with unbelievable speed, saved by Jay Pratt for these final seconds.

The Black was aiming straight ahead for the wire, but so were Flame and Apache! They raced toward the finish together, sweeping past the green and flowered infield garden. They were within fifty yards of the wire when Apache quit cold, leaving the Big Two to race it out.

The Black and Flame ran stride for stride, shoulder to shoulder, wild as a runaway team! From the stands there erupted a tremendous volume of sound, for it was an overwhelming end to a race that had already proved astonishing in its early speed, its saddle artistry and the courage of its horses. Now, with all that behind them, the champion and the foreign challenger were bringing down the curtain on the Widener in a dramatic rush that defied description. It was as if each horse had been loafing before. Each slammed along, ignoring the other alongside. It was a two-horse, two-jockey battle to the very last stride. It was a never forgotten struggle, and the shouts of the crowd rose to an unbelievable pitch as the two horses swept under the wire.

An unreal silence settled over the crowd. The Widener Handicap had ended but no one knew who the winner was. Only the official camera held the answer. All that mattered, at that particular moment, was that the world had witnessed one of the great races of history.

Another Day, Another Story

18

For the riders, too, it was a moment of silence. They straightened in their saddles but didn't stop their horses until midway around the first turn. Slowly, they cantered back. They'd had their share of glory in action and, for a few fleeting seconds, the thought of money was forgotten in favor of sentiment.

"You won a real race," Jay Pratt told Alec.

"I think Duncan got it," Alec answered.

"Maybe so," Pratt said. "And maybe Willy got home ahead of me. He came on again."

Willy Walsh rode alongside. "I belted him just once at the sixteenth pole and he took off. You should have seen him!"

"I didn't look back," Pratt said. "I just kept going."

Nick Marchione joined them. "I had a good shot at it," he said. "You can't ask for anything more than a good shot at something."

"I thought I was going to make it," Pete Edge said, "but he choked up on me. He couldn't breathe coming into the stretch. That's the only excuse I got."

They turned to Steve Duncan, who rode near them in silence.

"Your horse ran a million-dollar race, kid," Nick

Marchione called. "And you gave him a million-dollar ride."

Perhaps it was Nick's reference to money that caused their gazes to turn to the big infield board. The stewards were studying the pictures and any minute the results would be known. A lot of money hung in the balance: for first place, $87,700; second, $27,000; third, $13,500; and fourth, $6,800. The jockeys saw the winning time on the board and realized why those in the stands had started to jump with excitement. It was 1:58, breaking the American and world record for a mile and a quarter.

"I told you we were in a real big horse race," Nick Marchione said quietly, almost in awe.

The tremendous applause was for all of them as they jogged past the stands.

"Good ride, Nick!" someone on the rail screamed at the veteran jockey. "You rode like a starving apprentice!"

Nick Marchione grinned back. "Cheers today," he told Alec, "and jeers tomorrow. One day a hero and the next a bum. It never changes, huh, Alec?"

Then the numbers went up on the lighted board and the results of the Widener Handicap were officially known. The noise from the stands increased to a great roar. The camera had separated the Black and Flame and revealed the truth. The Black had won by the thinnest fraction of a nose! Following Flame's number 6 on the big board was number 1, Mad Wizard, so Willy Walsh had succeeded in bringing his mount on again to beat out Apache and Jay Pratt in those last few strides!

Alec saw a jubilant Henry Dailey waiting for him. Within a few minutes the Black would be in the winner's circle, wearing a wreath of flowers and not caring for it very much. He would be eager to get back to the barn and would kick out at those who pressed too closely to him. Then Henry would graciously, even modestly, accept the handsome Widener Cup. Alec knew how it would be, because it had all happened before.

The television cameras were on them, and the sportscaster walked alongside as Alec rode the Black into the circle. The sportscaster was telling his audience, "No racing fan with an ounce of blood in his veins could help but call this year's Widener one of the greatest epics of all time. It was easily the greatest race this reporter has ever seen or expects to see. It will, very probably, go down in the books as one of the greatest classics ever run on the American turf."

Alec glanced at the other horses leaving the track. They and their riders had made it a great race. And he felt that the activities about to take place in the winner's circle were not as important as his talking to Steve Duncan as soon as possible. For Steve, the apprentice rider, had been beaten to a greater extent than his horse.

Later, when the reporters had left the jockeys' room and the fanfare had ended, Alec found Steve alone on the far side of the room. He had changed to his street clothes and, it seemed to Alec, had been waiting for him.

"You know how it is now," Alec said. "One day they can't do enough for you and the next they don't even seem to know you're around. Sometimes you win by only a couple of inches but to reporters it makes all the difference in the world. Nick Marchione put it best: 'One day you're a hero, the next day a bum.' "

"I'm no bum," Steve said a little belligerently.

"I didn't mean it that way," replied Alec. "Nick didn't either. It's just a way we have of putting it. Forget it." He turned away, intending to leave. There was no sense in getting into any arguments with Steve. The Widener was already history.

"I got pushed around out there," Steve called after him.

Alec stopped and turned back to the boy. "Sure you did, but not as bad as you might have been. You did real well. What did you expect?"

"I had the fastest horse."

"Maybe and maybe not," Alec said slowly. "Every jock in every race thinks so. And the fastest horse doesn't always win. That's been proven, too."

"I was blocked six times. I counted them."

"You forget it the moment you cross the line," Alec said, "or you claim a foul. It's as simple as that." He paused before going on. "I'll tell you something else, Steve. What you call being blocked was only race-riding. No one's ever going to give you a clear path home unless you make it yourself."

"Yeah, but still—" Steve began, only to be interrupted angrily by Alec.

"You've got nothing to gripe about. You got second money and that, together with what you won in the Turf Cup, is more than you ever said you were after. But stick around, if more purse money is your goal now. You've got a real race horse in Flame; everybody knows it. And today you learned a lot more about race-riding than most jocks learn in a year. You have every opportunity to make all the money you want in this business. Just stick around."

For a moment Steve's eyes seemed troubled, even undecided, then he met Alec's gaze. "No," he said. "I'm not sticking around. I'm not interested in winning any more money. It's just that I think I could have beaten the Black. . . ."

Alec shrugged his shoulders. "Some other day, maybe. We'll be around, if you change your mind."

"No, there's not going to be another race day for me or Flame," Steve answered. "You've got one world, Alec. I have another."

"So go buy your island," Alec said with attempted lightness. He wanted to be friends with Steve, not bitter competitors. "As you say, we live in two different worlds."

"They're different, all right," Steve said. "Don't you like islands, Alec?"

"I was brought up on one," replied Alec, smiling. "Long Island. I don't believe, though, that it's much like yours."

Steve said, "You've never been surprised at my needing money to buy an island, Alec. Why?"

"Why should I be?" Alec asked in puzzlement. "I've got friends who bought an island in the St. Lawrence River, and others who bought them in the Bahamas." He paused, smiling. "Some paid even less than you're paying, Steve. So maybe you're not getting a bargain after all."

"I'm getting a bargain, all right," Steve answered quickly, the faraway look coming to his eyes. "Maybe you'd like to see it sometime," he added cautiously.

"Maybe," Alec answered.

Steve rose from his seat on the bench, extending a hand awkwardly. "Lots of luck, Alec. I'll keep track of what you do through the papers."

Alec shook the boy's hand. "But I won't know what you're up to, will I?" he asked.

"Not through the newspapers, anyway," Steve answered. "But I'll write."

"And I'll answer."

"Maybe someday I'll write you the whole story," Steve said. "There's a lot to tell you about Flame and my island. It'll read like a book."

"Then I've got a title for you," Alec said. "Make it *The Island Stallion.*"

"Yes," Steve said, "that's a good title. Maybe I'll use it someday."

Steve turned and walked away. Alec called, "Lots of luck, Steve."

The door to the jockeys' room closed behind Steve Duncan and Alec wondered if the boy ever would write a book about his horse and his island. He just might. He was that kind of guy. Hadn't he started all this with just a letter that no one would have believed?

Alec put away his racing silks for another day, anxious to get back to the Black Stallion and his own world of horses.

ABOUT THE AUTHOR

Walter Farley's love for horses began when he was a small boy living in Syracuse, New York, and continued as he grew up in New York City, where his family moved. Unlike most city children, he was able to fulfill this love through an uncle who was a professional horseman. Young Walter spent much of his time with this uncle, learning about the different kinds of horse training and the people associated with each.

Walter Farley began to write his first book, *The Black Stallion*, while he was a student at Brooklyn's Erasmus Hall High School and Mercersburg Academy in Pennsylvania. He finished it and had it published while he was still an undergraduate at Columbia University.

The appearance of *The Black Stallion* brought such an enthusiastic response from young readers that Mr. Farley went on to write more stories about the Black, and about other horses as well. He now has twenty-five books to his credit, including his first dog story, *The Great Dane Thor*, and his story of America's greatest thoroughbred, *Man o' War*. His books have been enormously successful in this country, and have also been published in fourteen foreign countries.

When not traveling, Walter Farley and his wife, Rosemary, divide their time between a farm in Pennsylvania and a beach house in Florida.